The Little Christmas Ornament

By Sharon Contillo

Illustrated by Steve Mardo

Copyright © 2014 Sharon M. Contillo

ISBN: 149751553X
ISBN-13: 978-1497515536

DEDICATION

To my T. On our very first Christmas we shared a special night decorating the tree, where every ornament had its special place. Who knew from that night this little story would be born. Thank you for always inspiring and encouraging me to follow my dreams and passions. This story is dedicated to you.

May all ornaments be seen!

CONTENTS

CONTENTS

ACKNOWLEDGMENTS

I wish to thank my daughters, Gillian and Mackenzie for their patience and understanding while I typed away, creating this story. I write stories because my mind won't let me stop. I make them the best they can be because of you.

To my parents, Janice and Ron, thank you for always encouraging me and allowing me to have no fear of failure. Our young family inspired me to recreate the family and setting in this story. I'm truly the luckiest to have you as parents.

This book would not have been possible without the guidance, direction and impassioned support of my mentor, Chris Soth. Words cannot express my gratitude for your befitting counsel, professionalism and really good humor! You are a gifted storyteller.

To David Wisehart for helping me adapt this from screenplay to chapter book. Your direction and guidance was professional and spot on!

To my Editor Kathryn Ward, thank you for guiding me through this process. I am extremely grateful for your encouragement and endless professional advice.

And to my Illustrator, Steve Mardo, you are extremely talented, a very generous and patient artist. Thank you for the countless sketches and having exceptionally skilled hands for bringing my vision to life.

CHAPTER 1

It wasn't long ago or in some far away land, but it was a dark and mysterious place. A place where no human had ever been, at least not that any Christmas ornament or light bulb could remember. It's the inside of a Christmas tree!

In the magical world of a Christmas tree, the ornaments and light bulbs are alive. Some are on the front of the tree, some are on the sides, and some are on the back. As the saying goes, "The grass is always greener on the other side," so naturally all the back ornaments want to be on the front.

A Christmas tree not only has many sides and many levels, it also has lots of gloomy places near the trunk where the Christmas light bulbs don't shine and the light of day never peeks in. No one wants to be in these places—they are too frightening and dark.

Billy ran through this darkness. He was not a fast runner. His short legs were made of Styrofoam painted to look like the legs of a gingerbread man. Most of the time, Billy liked looking like a gingerbread man, with his painted arms and legs and his green plaid vest and bow tie.

But now someone wanted to take a bite of him—or worse, throw him from the tree to his death! That someone was gaining on him. And it had big yellow eyes and a large snout.

Billy could hear the rustle and crack of tree branches moving behind him and the rough, heavy sound of someone breathing hard. He could feel hot breath at the back of his neck, but Billy didn't dare turn around to get a good look.

Run! he thought, scared and panicky.

He raced as fast as he could along the tree limbs, jumping from branch to branch. It was slippery and dangerous. Billy was now deep inside the tree where there weren't many ornaments or light bulbs. He passed a paper snowflake that had been folded one time or maybe even hundreds. He passed a cardboard candy cane with its edges turned up, worn and crumpled, and an old pixie elf with its nose broken off. They eyed Billy, wondering what he was doing deep inside the tree.

He peeked down as he ran; it was a long way to the hardwood floor and the braided rug below.

Don't fall! he warned himself.

Yellow Eyes was getting closer. That evil snouted beast wouldn't give up. *Maybe I should have stayed in my spot,* Billy thought. But in his heart he felt he had to take a chance and escape, for he was afraid to stay in his usual spot on the back of the tree.

Billy's spot was on the very end of a tree branch, tucked in the corner of the room—a place where ornaments mysteriously disappeared, and a place where no humans ever saw him. Like all ornaments, Billy wanted to be seen; he longed to be admired and smiled at by the humans.

That was an ornament's purpose—to bring Christmas spirit to the family.

But the back of the tree had few ornaments and light bulbs and for good reason. Humans couldn't get their hands back there. And why bother, for no one saw those ornaments anyway; they were simply filler. Filler ornaments and light bulbs were only on the tree to make it seem full to anyone looking at the tree from the sides.

Billy had had enough of being on the back. He wanted to be safe. And he longed to be part of the team that truly brings Christmas spirit. But Billy was now running for his life, and as he ran, a worried thought filled his head: *Where the heck am I going?*

He could see a light in front of him. Billy knew it was always brighter on the outside of the tree, and darker on the inside near the trunk. *If I run for the light,* he thought, *I'll get to the end of a branch and I'll be able to see where I am.* But there were so many branches, and none of the ones near Billy looked familiar at all. Neither did any of the ornaments who stared at him sternly, clearly upset that an ornament from the back of the tree was trying to sneak forward to a better spot.

Completely out of breath Billy realized, *I'm lost.* This thought worried him terribly, more than anything ever had. All these branches were completely new to him, and any of these ornaments could simply push him from the tree if they thought he was out of place. Ornaments were very protective of their spots, especially if the spots were good ones.

His legs were getting tired and shaky. It seemed like he had been running a very long time, and he was tired from tip to toe. *Don't fall.* Just as he was thinking that, his

Styrofoam feet slipped from the tree branch and he fell with a sudden, heart-stopping drop. He felt his stomach rise into his throat.

Oh, no!

As Billy fell, he reached out with his Styrofoam hands, but his rounded mitts couldn't grab anything. He kept falling. Billy hit another branch below him, bounced off it to one side, and felt his head jerk. Before Billy knew what happened, he was dangling in the air.

My hook!

All the Christmas tree ornaments had hooks on their heads. Luckily Billy's had caught on a branch. *I'm safe,* he thought. But he heard the sound of twigs snapping behind him.

Yellow Eyes!

Billy reached up and awkwardly grabbed the branch above him with his rounded Styrofoam mitts. With one mitt he unhooked himself, and he swung from branch to branch. As he did, the other ornaments and light bulbs watched him. They were probably thinking this was some new agility-training program to keep ornaments in shape during the Christmas season.

Billy saw a branch beneath him and let go of the one above. He landed on the lower branch and began to run again, faster and faster. Large Christmas light bulbs lit the way. It was a good sign. *Almost there.*

At last, he reached an opening. But something slipped over his head, and he felt himself yanked back.

Thud!

He fell and landed on a bed of sharp pine needles. He looked down at his Styrofoam body and saw he'd been lassoed by a tiny plastic wreath made of fake plastic light bulbs.

"Ha! Ha! Ha!" Billy heard the evil snort of Yellow

Eyes bellowing in triumph.

Desperate, Billy yanked a sharp pine needle from a tree branch.

"Yeow, put that back!" someone said.

Who's that? thought Billy, but then he decided, *No time to question anything—time to act!*

A pink plastic snout emerged from the darkness. *Yellow Eyes!*

Billy raised the pine needle to defend himself. He closed his eyes and jammed it straight into that pink snout so hard that it bent.

Yellow Eyes squealed in pain, "Oink! Oink!"

Billy watched as the wounded pink-snouted ornament slipped back into the darkness. He tossed away the bent pine needle, stood up, stepped out of the wreath, and leapt over a branch. Then all of a sudden—

Smack!

"Ugh," he said.

He bounced back onto the prickly tree branch, thinking, *What was that?* He peered up into the branches, and he found himself looking into two deep dark eyes.

It was Lo, a clear glass ball ornament with a furry purple teddy bear head that had become matted with age. Her soft brown eyes gave a cute cub-like appearance. A golden halo circled above her head. Chipped golden wings hung off the back of her glass ball. Stuffed purple paws—short and stubby—jutted out in front of her. They held a tiny clipboard and a pen. She had no legs to stand on, but she could swing from her hook to move from branch to branch.

She was the leader of all the ornaments, and now she hovered over Billy.

"Hello, Billy," she said.

"Rats!" said Billy.

"Foiled again?"

"I was almost there!"

Lo extended her short worn paw, reaching down to help Billy stand up. "Mmm-hmm," she said. As she murmured, she scanned the inside of the tree and made checkmarks on her tiny clipboard.

Billy began to plead with her. "C'mon, Lo. Please let me be on the front. The guests are coming any minute and—"

"Whoa, Billy. The guests aren't due until tomorrow."

"Tomorrow?" Billy was suddenly confused. "I thought the party was today."

"Nope. See . . ." Lo pointed into the parlor of the house.

Billy looked where she was pointing, and he saw an object propped on the television console.

"What's that?" he asked.

"That," said Lo, "is an Advent calendar."

"What's an Advent calendar?"

"It tells the day of the Christmas month."

Billy didn't understand, but he nodded anyway.

Lo continued. "See those open cardboard windows?"

"Yeah, I see them."

"Notice how all the cardboard windows are cracked open except for three?"

Billy saw numbers on the closed windows. He knew his numbers, and he read them out loud: "Twenty-three, twenty-four, twenty-five."

Lo nodded. "Those are the days that haven't happened yet. December twenty-third is the day of the party. And that's tomorrow."

Putting it together in his head, Billy realized his mistake. "Ugh . . . I made my break too early."

"You did."

"Lo, please, for old time's sake. Can I please be on the front?"

Lo shook herself. "I'm sorry, Billy. We all have our spots." She spun him toward the back. "Now, no more escaping from the back."

"Lo, you have no idea what it's like back there! No one sees you and . . . and . . . it's creepy scary! I think Yellow Eyes—"

"Who?" Lo asked.

"I mean, Flying Pig," he said, correcting himself. Then he blurted out, "I think Flying Pig made it on the tree this year! He's kicking ornaments off the back! To their death!"

Lo studied her clipboard. "Hmm. Nope, I don't see Flying Pig listed here. It's okay, Billy. You're safe."

Billy didn't feel safe. And he didn't want to go back to his old spot. He didn't like it in the back of the tree.

"Aw, Lo, I wish I were pretty or glitzy or something special like you, so I could be on the front, too."

Lo smiled. She wanted everyone to feel special, and so she gave her clipboard another glance. "Billy, you know what?" Her voice was suddenly upbeat. "Christmas Mouse didn't make it on the tree this year, so I do have an opening on the side."

He felt a sudden thrill run through him from his Styrofoam head to his Styrofoam toes. "Really?" But a worry gripped him. He knew toy soldiers patrolled the sides, keeping back ornaments from sneaking to the front. They always marched together in a group, intimidating the other ornaments. "It's not near the toy soldiers, is it?"

"Nope."

He sighed with relief. "Then I'll take it!"

Lo's matted paw caressed his shoulder. "Billy, listen.

Every ornament on this tree is important, no matter where it hangs. And I need you and everyone else to help make this our most beautiful Christmas tree ever. Got it?"

Billy nodded happily. "Got it."

Then he followed Lo to find his new place on the side of the tree.

CHAPTER 2

Lo swung up higher on the tree, moving from branch to branch. She caught each new limb of the seven-foot Douglas fir by the hook on the top of her head and swung up again, released the branch, and caught the next one. It was fun moving around the tree, but she had to be careful not to move too far from her own assigned place. The humans in the house didn't know that the ornaments could move, and Lo wasn't going to be the one to shatter their illusions. If she heard footsteps, or a door opening, or the sound of a car parking outside, it was back to her spot immediately.

As she went higher, branch by branch, Lo passed the many colorful Christmas ornaments that hung from every branch.

A spot for every ornament, thought Lo, *and every ornament in its spot.*

She acknowledged the others as she moved by. Nearest to her, a tiny elf twirled on a hook. The elf was dressed in green and red, with little booties and a cheery smile. "Hello, Pixie!" Lo said, not wanting to pause for a long conversation but not wanting to be rude, either.

"Hello, Lo!"

Pixie is always in a merry mood, Lo thought. This was more than Lo could say for some of the other ornaments. Pixie knew her place and believed it was the perfect spot for her. She'd hung on that same branch every Christmas for the last five years. That branch suited her just fine. Lo couldn't imagine a better spot for Pixie.

Moving up to the next branch, Lo passed a spinning top painted bright shades of blue and yellow. "Hello, Top!"

"Hello, Lo!" he said with dizzy eyes.

Bicycle Santa straddled a bike, pedaling fast but going nowhere. His little wheels spun in the air beneath him as he dangled from his branch. He was in a merry mood today, too. "Hello, Bicycle Santa!"

"Hello, Lo! Can I take you for a spin?"

"Some other time, Santa. Some other time."

Two penguins popped out of a tiny Christmas stocking. They were dressed in their fine penguin tuxes and playing cards. "Hello, Penguins!"

"Hello, Lo."

"Good luck with the game."

There were Christmas balls of many colors and sizes. They all bounced happily on their branches.

Just up above was the choo-choo train, Chooch. He tried to blow his smoke stack. *He knows better,* Lo thought, and she swung up to his branch. "Hey, Chooch," she said. "No smoking, right?"

"Hunh?" Chooch was slow and dopey.

Lo shook her head and tapped the branch they were both hanging from. "Flammable."

Chooch looked up at the branch. His eyes opened

wide, and his face turned bright red. "Oh, right, Lo."

Lo winked and patted Chooch's caboose.

Leaving him hanging there, motionless and confused, Lo propped herself up where all the lights and ornaments could see her, and she began her speech. "Okay, folks! Not much time left, so let's make sure we're all shiny and bright. We are hosting this year's Christmas tree contest party—"

The other ornaments protested, "Aw, no . . ."

Lo continued. "C'mon. It'll be fun. Especially because this year we're going to win!"

No response.

"Right?" Lo asked. "Right?"

Some of them grumbled.

Lo sensed little support from the ornaments and lights. They needed convincing. "Think of how great it'll feel when they announce us as the winners!" She slid down a string of lights to a tiny gold ball and looked at her own distorted reflection in the glass. "Then we'll get what we've always wanted." She peered up and saw blank stares from the ornaments. She turned to the little train. "Chooch, help me out here. What is it we all want?"

Chooch looked confused. "Uh, coal?"

Laughter shook the branches of the Christmas tree.

But Lo did not laugh. This was a serious matter.

"Coal?" she said. "No! Coal is for naughty people—and steam trains." The laughter started again, but Lo silenced everyone with a stern look. Then she softened, remembering to smile, and she said, "We all want to be looked at. Admired. Right? We've waited all year for this!"

Some of the ornaments nodded, twirled, or spoke in agreement: "Oh, yeah." "Yes." "Right!"

Lo sensed the enthusiasm building, and she added to their Christmas excitement. "We'll be the envy of the neighborhood! And we, my fellow ornamentals, will bring the most Christmas spirit to our family!" She stretched her paws out wide. Her chin rose with pride, and she closed her eyes, anticipating a round of applause. But she got nothing.

"We don't stand a chance," said a green metal ornament shaped like a pickle. He was always pessimistic and gloomy.

Lo's mood sank, as it usually did when Pickle spoke.

"The Monroes win every year," Pickle added, bringing down the mood for everyone.

"Well, Pickle," said Lo, "not this year. I have carefully placed everyone to ensure our ultimate victory." She studied her clipboard, comparing the current arrangement of the ornaments with her precise and detailed plans.

Pickle interrupted her thoughts. "Yeah, maybe you should revisit that?"

"We're unbeatable," Lo insisted.

But Pickle only frowned with annoyance at a sleeping dwarf-like ornament called Gnome who was hanging too close so he pushed Gnome, waking him.

In a crotchety voice, Gnome said, "Hey! Watch it!"

Pickle scowled. "You're too close, troll."

"I'm not a troll, I'm a gnome!" He pushed Pickle back.

Lo, dreaming of victory in the Christmas tree competition, didn't notice their squabble. "We'll win this contest," she said proudly. "We'll be named the most beautiful, sparkling tree in the neighborhood. We'll bring Christmas spirit to our family! All we have to do is work together!"

Pickle shoved Gnome again. "You're as ugly as a troll. How did you make it on the tree?"

Gnome narrowed his gnomish eyes, wrinkled his

gnomish face, and tackled Pickle.

Lo was still preoccupied with her clipboard, but the other ornaments watched as Pickle and Gnome wrestled. They plummeted, and *thwack!*—they hit the branch Lo was dangling from. The branch sprang back into place and flung Lo to a higher branch.

She caught her hook on it, and found herself face to face with, Smiley, another ornament, who was frowning. "I need a smile on that face, Smiley."

In a low voice Smiley replied, "Just resting my cheeks, Lo." Then he rehearsed his smile.

She nodded. "Great, Smiley! Keep it up." Lo liked encouraging the others. It made her feel like the excellent team leader she knew she was.

As she looked around, she noticed Snowman twirling gently and watching the colored lights reflect off of his glitzy coating. Suddenly he twisted face forward, eyes wide, as if in shock: "Red alert! Red alert!"

Lo knew that a red alert could mean only one thing—*the family!*

She spun forward and scanned the parlor. She didn't see any signs of humans, but heard their footsteps: three sets of sounds, which meant three humans. One sounded much heavier than the others: *one adult—the father—and the two children.*

Lo turned back to the ornaments. "Hold still, everyone! Don's coming in with the kids!"

Pickle and Gnome stopped wrestling. The other ornaments froze.

Lo leaped across several branches, passing Billy, who encouraged her onward. "Hurry, Lo! You can make it!"

She latched onto a string of lights and slid into her place in the front and center of the tree. She glanced at Belle, a shiny blue bell ornament, and checked herself in the reflection of Belle's shiny body. "How am I looking, Belle?"

Belle answered with her proper Louisiana drawl, "You're lookin' mighty fine, Miss Lo."

Lo winked a *thank you*.

The front ornaments watched motionlessly as three humans entered the parlor. Just as Lo thought, it was Don and the kids. Don was a young man with neat dark hair parted on the side. Today he wore a sweater vest and neatly polished shoes. With him were Gina and Ronnie. Gina was six years old with soft brown curly hair; tonight she wore a pink flannel bathrobe. Ronnie was seven years old with a mop top haircut; he was wearing racing car pajamas.

"What's Don up to?" she wondered aloud, keeping her voice to a whisper so the humans wouldn't hear.

Pickle swung into his spot above Lo. "I'll tell you what he's up to—no good!"

"Mr. Pickle," said Belle, "don't be so sour." She peeked through the branches. "Why, they're just lookin' out the window."

"It's probably snowing," said Lo.

"I don't think so," said Pickle. "Starlight says there's no snow. Santa's going to be riding in on wheels this year."

"Let's go see," said Belle.

Lo peered into the parlor. "Okay, but let's make this quick in case Janice comes in."

Together Lo, Belle, and Pickle climbed to the top of the tree. There they met up with the glowing star-shaped tree topper, Starlight. "I didn't expect you three," said Starlight in her deep, soothing voice.

Pickle said, "Don is up to something."

"It's nothing," said Starlight without a hint of worry. "They're looking at a tree across the street."

Lo felt a shiver run through her. *They should be looking*

at us. We're the best tree in the neighborhood. "Checking out our competition?" Lo asked.

"No," answered Starlight. "See for yourself. Look there, in the third-story window."

Lo, Belle, and Pickle looked out over the heads of the humans and through the nearby bay window. They could overhear what the family was saying.

"Way cool," Ronnie said. "Are we getting one?"

"We sure are," said Don.

Pickle leaned in and whispered to Lo, "Getting one? Getting one what?"

Lo squinted, casting her gaze across the street. She saw the three-story house on the other side. It was wedged tightly between two other three-story houses. Inside the house, and visible through the third-story window, was a sparkling aluminum Christmas tree. The tree rotated slowly, shining brightly. Red, green, yellow, and blue lights washed over it. Lo gasped. So did the others.

Belle was the first to speak. "Goodness me, I've never seen anything like that."

"Me neither," said Pickle. "It's . . . beautiful."

Belle seemed offended. "I beg to differ, Mr. Pickle."

"Hush," said Lo, listening to the humans.

"But Daddy," Gina was saying, "Where are the lights? The ornaments?"

"That's the beauty of it, Gina." Don smiled at her. "There aren't any tangled lights and old dull ornaments."

Lo was astonished. *"Old dull ornaments?" Is he talking about us?*

"That sparkling silver Christmas tree spins slowly," Don continued, "around and around."

Lo tested the idea, spinning on her hook around and around, but she felt dizzy, and stopped. *That's no good.*

"On the floor," Don explained, "are these neat

rotating wheels with colored panels. Together they shine different colors onto the spinning tree, so you can see different shades of red, green, yellow, and blue."

"That's so cool," said Ronnie

"Not cool at all," whispered Pickle.

"Hush," Lo said again.

"It sure is cool," Don agreed. "And Daddy won't have to untangle the pesky lights and pack and repack the ugly old ornaments. We can just plug this one in."

"Let's get one." Ronnie said. "We'll win the Christmas tree contest for sure."

Lo shook her head. *They can't be serious.*

Don answered, "We sure will!"

"But Daddy," Gina said, "what about our ornaments and lights?"

"We can just throw them out. We won't need them."

And with that, Lo felt her heart sink as low as it could possibly go.

CHAPTER 3

An aluminum Christmas tree? With no ornaments and light strings? Lo didn't like the sound of that.

And it didn't make sense. Christmas trees were supposed to be real trees that you could touch and smell and hang ornaments and lights on, like the wonderful Douglas fir that Lo was dangling from right now, or the Scotch pine from last year, or the blue spruce from a few years before. They all smelled like Christmas. All the trees Lo had ever known had been real trees. She knew that some families had fake trees, but those never won the Christmas tree contest. How could they? Real trees with ornaments and Christmas lights went together like warm cookies with cold milk. It was the way things had always been, and the way things should always be.

"He's going to throw us out!" Pickle said, keeping his voice low so as not to be heard by the human family in the parlor.

"That won't happen," whispered Lo, but she wasn't as sure as she sounded. "That shiny thing is not a

Christmas tree! You can't have a Christmas tree without ornaments and lights. Janice would never stand for it."

She heard a human voice in another room, the sound of a woman saying, "Kids?"

Janice, Lo thought. Janice was the mother of the human family, the one who bought a new real Christmas tree every year, who draped each string of lights just right to give the tree the best lighting, who hung the ornaments carefully. And she was the one who placed them ever so gently back in their comfy ornament boxes when Christmas was over. *Janice loves everything about Christmas trees and ornaments.*

Don, Gina, and Ronnie continued to stare across the street at the aluminum tree shining colorfully in its third-story window. Their backs were turned to Lo, and they couldn't see what was happening on their own tree. Don and the kids never really noticed when the ornaments changed places, but Janice would notice. She did most of the work deciding the placement of the ornaments, and she would know if any had moved. She had noticed once or twice before, so Lo had taken it upon herself always to check the tree before Janice found any mistakes. It was Lo's job to keep the ornaments in their right spots and to make sure they didn't move around too much or talk above a whisper when humans were near. If the humans learned that the ornaments and lights could talk, that would ruin Christmas spirit forever. So it must be kept a secret.

Lo double-checked the tree and noticed that some of ornaments, including herself, Belle, and Pickle, were out of place. They had moved from their spots to look out the window. And now Janice was on her way into the parlor.

Pickle whispered, "Hurry!"

As Janice's footsteps came closer, Lo, Belle, and Pickle moved in a mad panic to return to their proper places. Lo saw her branch, but Pickle was in the way.

Move, Pickle! Deciding to go over him, Lo swung to a higher branch and just missed crashing into Belle. *Out of my way!* she thought, but she dare not speak with humans in the room.

Janice's footsteps came closer.

Lo stared at her spot, directly below her. She released her hook from the upper branch and dropped down, but out of nowhere Pickle appeared, moving into her way again. *Smack!*—Lo bumped him, hard, nearly bouncing off the tree. But just in time she caught the branch with her hook.

Ow, thought Lo, as Belle and Pickle returned to their spots on the front of the tree.

Lo was swinging back and forth. She tried to stop as Janice stepped in the room and turned to the Christmas tree. Some ornaments were still shaking, but Janice didn't notice. She was staring straight at Lo, who was still swinging.

Don't mind me, Lo thought. *Nothing unusual. It's just the wind. These old houses are drafty, and breezes can blow in and set an ornament in motion.*

Janice reached her hand out to Lo and steadied her, and she leaned her human face forward, kissing Lo's little teddy bear head.

"My sweet little ornament," she said.

Gina turned away from the window and joined Janice by the tree.

"Mama," said Gina, "you're kissing an ornament?"

"Of course," her mother replied. "This is my very first ornament. I love her. Nana gave her to me when I was a little girl."

"Can I see her?"

Janice lifted Gina up and brought her to eye-level

with Lo.

Lo gazed straight ahead, frozen, struggling not to move.

Janice said, "She's my teddy bear angel. I hang her front and center on our tree every year."

"Why?"

"Because she is my favorite ornament, and I want everyone to see her."

Gina reached out and stroked Lo's head with her little hand. Gold specks flicked off Lo's angel wings.

Easy there, Lo thought. *I can't grow those back.*

The little girl said, "Can I hold her?"

No, no, no, please, no.

"No, honey," Janice said.

Lo sighed in relief.

"She's extremely fragile. We have to be very careful with her. Nana looks forward to seeing her on our tree every year. So let's keep her safe and sound, okay?"

Janice lowered the girl, and Gina sank out of Lo's sight.

Whew! Thanks, Janice. She's a sweet kid, but her hands are more suited for something made of rubber.

Gina said, "Mama, I don't want to throw her out."

Lo felt a quick panic. *Don't even mention that!*

"Throw her out?" Janice asked. "Why would we do that?"

"Daddy says we're going to throw out all the ornaments and lights and get a spinning silver tree."

With these words, the entire Christmas tree shuddered with fear from the trembling of the frightened lights and ornaments. But they were relieved by Janice's reply.

"Daddy is dreaming, honey. I would never throw out our ornaments and lights, especially my precious little ornament. What would we look at?"

As she spoke, Janice lovingly touched a few other ornaments. Lo felt a twinge of jealousy, but she comforted herself with the knowledge that she was Janice's favorite.

"It just wouldn't be Christmas," Janice continued, cupping Lo in her hand. "Our tree is so beautiful this year. I can't wait for everyone to see it."

"Me, too," said Gina.

"Come with me, sweetie, I have something for you."

As Gina and Janice moved away, Lo heard their footsteps fade. Checking the window, she saw that Don and Ronnie had also left the room. She sighed with relief. "Great job, everyone! That was perfect!" She turned to Pickle. "See, no one's getting thrown out. Now let's win this contest and show Don that he's wrong about that silver tree." She pulled out her clipboard and reviewed her checkmarks.

Pickle said, "Oh, no . . ."

Lo gave him a look. "What?" As she did, she heard Gina's voice as Janice and Gina returned.

"Yay!" Gina had something in her hand.

Janice's fingers touched one of the branches, unhooked Belle, and moved Belle down to a lower branch.

Belle whispered, "Gracious me, no!"

Lo felt helpless. *What's going on? Why is she moving ornaments around? This can't be good.*

Gina's little hand hung something next to Lo, but Lo didn't dare turn to look at it.

A new ornament? she thought.

Suddenly, a stray lock of blond hair from the new ornament fluttered in Lo's face. "Pfft!" Lo sputtered. She glanced sideways. The new ornament looked like a pretty female doll with long platinum-blond hair parted in the middle. The doll wore white go-go boots and a dress you could almost see through. A bell hung off a pull string at the ornament's back, along with a tag that was stamped with a name: "HOLLY."

"Now everyone can see her, right?" Gina was saying.

"Right, sweetie. Now you have your very own special ornament to hang on the tree every year, just like me."

"Can they hang next to each other every year, Mama?"

"Sure they can."

Every year? Horrified, Lo glanced again at the newcomer, Holly.

But the newcomer didn't glance back at her. Instead, Holly's painted-on smile and unblinking eyes only stared straight ahead, ignoring Lo and everyone else on the tree.

CHAPTER 4

Morning came. In just a few hours it would be time for the big party and the Christmas tree competition. Lo knew better than anyone how important tonight was for the ornaments and the lights. She feared that if they didn't win the this contest, they'd all be replaced by an aluminum tree, just like the one that even now rotated endlessly, lit by red, green, yellow, and blue lights, in the third-story window across the street. But if they won the contest, Janice would surely get her way, and the lights and ornaments would survive to be on a live tree in the family's parlor every Christmas, forever.

Lo had another big problem—the one right next her. The new ornament, Holly, was hanging too close. Lo felt trapped and wanted to find another place for the newcomer. But she couldn't do anything at that moment because Gina was standing on a wooden child's chair and playing with the ornaments like dolls.

I'm not a doll, Lo wanted to remind the little girl. *I'm fragile. I can break.* Lo feared that at any moment the child would drop her.

Gina stroked Holly's hair, and she twisted Lo and Holly to face each other, giving Lo her first really good look at the intruder.

She's much prettier than me, Lo realized, and her heart sank.

Now Gina was playing with the ornaments as if they were puppets, jiggling them and talking for them.

In a high-pitched voice as she waggled Holly, Gina said, "Hello, my name is Holly. What's yours?"

And in a lower-pitched voice, Gina replied, "I'm Mama's Little Ornament."

That doesn't sound like me at all, Lo thought.

"Want to be my friend?" Gina said in her Holly voice.

"I'd like that," she said in the Lo voice. "You can hang next to me every Christmas, Holly."

No!

"Yay!" said the Holly voice.

Gina pulled the string on Holly's back and the buttons on her dress lit up in red and green. Then Gina made Holly and Lo hug each other.

Lo's eyes rolled. *Please, someone, make her stop.*

"Friends forever." Gina unhooked Holly and rehooked her onto Lo's branch.

That's too close, thought Lo. *We need space, little girl, space.* She almost said it out loud.

Gina pressed Holly and Lo together. "Perfect!" She hopped down from the chair and left the room.

When Lo was sure Gina was gone, she said to Holly, "Ah-hem. Maybe you can hop over a branch to make this a little more comfortable for both of us?"

Holly stared, sneered, and pursed her lips. "Like, maybe *you* should hop over to another branch," she said in a sassy voice.

Looking on, some of the other ornaments murmured, "Ooo . . ."

Tell me she just didn't say that, Lo thought. She wasn't used to being challenged. But she smiled at Holly. "Ha ha. That's very funny. But, ah, this is my spot."

"Oh?" said Holly. "We have spots?"

"Of course, we have spots. If we didn't have spots, there would be clumping and chaos on the tree."

"So what?"

"We don't want clumping." She nudged Holly and held her straight out, so that Holly's body was parallel with the floor. "And we don't want chaos."

"Why?"

"Because tonight is the big contest."

In spite of her position being held sideways in Lo's grasp, Holly brightened. "A contest? I love competition!" Then to Smiley, Holly said, "I won 'Prettiest off the Assembly Line.'"

Smiley frowned and blinked, saying nothing.

But Pickle spoke up. "I bet you did." He seemed impressed.

Lo rolled her eyes. *How can anyone stand her? Those boots, that dress, and especially that attitude. So what if she's pretty? Pretty isn't everything.*

Belle spoke up. "You may have been 'Prettiest off the Assembly Line,' but Lo is the prettiest and most special ornament on this tree."

The front ornaments nodded in unison, and Lo blushed.

But Holly only looked around her. "Lo? Who's Lo?"

"That would be me," Lo said.

"Ha! You?" Holly looked at Lo, casting her gaze up and down.

Lo's face warmed with embarrassment.

Holly continued, "I'm thinking . . . no. To Lo." She elbowed Smiley. "Ha, right? Am I right?"

No one spoke.

"Get it?" Holly said. "'No to Lo?'" She frowned at the lack of response. "What a dull tree." She looked around at the other ornaments, who seemed unimpressed. "A plain gold ball and a candy cane? What? No hunky lumberjacks on this tree?"

Lo scowled. She released Holly, unable to hold her out any longer.

Holly slammed into Lo. Then she composed herself and flicked her hair, which hit Lo in the mouth.

"Ugh!" Lo cried and spat out Holly's hair. "Pfft!"

But Holly ignored her.

Lo examined her clipboard mumbling, "Hunky lumberjacks? On a tree? Yeah, that's smart." Looking down, Lo spotted Chooch. "Ah, Chooch? Why don't you move one branch over to the left, so you can hang more freely?"

"Gotcha, Lo." The train ornament chugged to his new branch.

Lo examined the side of the tree and saw a bare spot that needed to be filled. "Otto, please move two branches to the right."

Otto was a 1960s flower-power-style Volkswagen bus. He revved his engine and said in a German accent, "Ja! Zoom, zoom!" as he peeled out and motored over to his new spot on a branch next to Billy.

Holly watched all this, and then she spoke to Lo. "What are you doing?"

"Maximizing our sparkle."

"That's a bit controlling."

Lo turned to the others. "C'mon, folks. Let's make this snappy. We have to win this contest. Let's not give

Don a reason to throw anybody out!"

The ornaments shuddered, "Ooo, no!"

"Happy and merry! That's what I want to see," Lo said.

The ornaments nodded. They checked their smiles and their shines, and they spiffed themselves up.

But Holly was unconvinced of Lo's leadership. "I think we should hang wherever we want."

Lo was shocked. "What?"

"It feels more free."

At these words, some ornaments began to whirl with excitement.

"Maybe Holly's got a point," said Pickle.

"See," said Holly. "I've got a point. Power to the ornaments. Spread the love." She flashed a peace sign with her tiny fingers.

Lo felt her anger rise. "Are you crazy?" *Oops, too loud.* She lowered her voice to a whisper. "If you keep saying that, the back ornaments will charge to the front."

"So what?" Holly shouted so everyone could hear.

Lo gritted her teeth. "Would you please keep it down?" She eyed the back of the tree where, somewhere in the darkness, she heard the shadowy figures as they rustled. "If the ornaments think they can hang wherever they want, there'll be mayhem!"

Holly laughed. "Bring 'em all to the front. The more, the merrier! That's what we're trying to accomplish, right? Happiness? Merriness? Christmas spirit?"

She looked around for support, and several of the front ornaments nodded in approval.

I'm losing them, Lo thought. "Yes, of course, Christmas spirit is important," she said. "But right now the back ornaments need to stay in the back. We need to win this contest."

"That seems a little mean. So much for the halo." As Holly spoke, she reached out a tiny hand and flicked Lo's halo.

"Watch it!" said Lo. "It could break."

"And then what happens? You come down to earth?"

"My halo is my direct link to Santa."

Holly began to laugh, shaking in a fit of hilarity. "Oh, oh, oh—you've got to stop. You are too much! First, you're the prettiest and most special, and now a direct link to Santa? You're killing me, Bear!"

Belle spoke up in Lo's defense, "Why, Miss Lo can absolutely talk to Santa. She's an angel."

"And now an angel!" Holly burst out in laughter again. "Is there no limit to you?" She caught her breath and turned to the front ornaments. "Hmm, okay. Let's see if this thing works." She grabbed Lo's halo, pulled it toward her like a microphone, and spoke into it. "Hello, Santa? Come in, Santa." She put her ear to the halo. "What? Speak louder, Santa, I can't hear you."

Excited, Chooch cried out, "It's Santa!"

The front ornaments nodded eagerly.

Holly continued. "What's that, Santa? Lo's a big fat liar?"

The ornaments murmured with shocked amazement.

"Stop that!" Lo straightened her halo.

But Holly grabbed it again and pretended again to speak to Santa. "Don't worry, I'll make sure we're ready. You can count on me, Santa. See you on Christmas Eve!" Holly released the halo and smirked, "Ha! A plastic halo."

Lo heard ornaments whispering: "It's plastic?" "I don't know." "Maybe it is . . ."

"It doesn't matter!" Lo cried. "It doesn't matter what it's made of. It doesn't."

The front ornaments grumbled in response.

They don't believe me, thought Lo. "It's a real halo," she insisted. "I'm not lying!"

But Holly twirled her finger by the side of her head, making the crazy sign. "Don't listen to Lo," she said to everyone on the tree. "Hang wherever you want."

The front ornaments looked at each other, wondering who should make the first move. Pixie Elf dropped to a lower branch—a better spot. Next a blue robin ornament moved. Soon everyone was moving up or down or sideways.

"Come on, it's great!" someone said, as the front ornaments rallied the others from the sides and the bottom. They all surged forward, storming the front of the tree.

"No! Wait! You'll tip the tree!" Lo cried.

But everyone ignored her.

"That's it," Holly said. "Do your own thing! Hang wherever you want!"

"Yeah," Pickle said, "wherever we want!"

Pickle shoved Gnome, who did a loop-the-loop.

"Be free!" said Holly. "Spread the love!"

The ornaments took up the chant: "Spread the love! Spread the love!"

How did I lose control of them so fast? What's happening? This is terrible! Lo felt betrayed as she tried to stop them. "No!"

Holly grinned, pleased with herself.

Now the ornaments were jostling around, bumping into each other.

Lo was pushed deeper into the tree. "I can talk to Santa!" she protested, "I can."

But no one was listening.

CHAPTER 5

Lo was too far inside to the tree to see what was happening on the outer branches, but from what she could hear and feel, she knew there was complete chaos. She heard ornaments fighting and jostling for position. The entire tree shook with the tug and tussle. Arguments were rampant.

"That's my spot," said someone.

"Oh, yeah?" said another. "I look better right here!"

"Why do I have to be down here?"

"This is a wonderful view," someone else said happily. "I like this much better."

"Move aside."

"Watch it!"

"Watch it yourself!"

"But where do I go?"

"Go wherever you want!" cried Holly from her spot in the front and center. "Do whatever you want."

Knowing she had to take action, Lo climbed from branch to branch toward the top, struggling through the gloomy inner part of the tree. It was darker inside, but as she reached the top it got lighter, and eventually she was able to poke her head up into the light. From the top, she peeked out the window.

The sun is setting, she thought. *This has gone on for too long. I have to do something.*

She headed back down the tree to her usual spot, but with everyone in different positions, she had a hard time figuring out where to go and how to get there. She pushed past Pixie to get a better view of the front.

Looking down, she could see ornaments clumped together on her branch. It drooped with the extra weight.

"That's my spot. You need to go back your own!" she shouted.

But no one could hear her over the commotion.

She looked around for friends and allies. Pickle polished himself with a scarf from an elf ornament. Tug Boat twisted left and right, while Snowman and Bicycle Santa judged which side was better and gave a thumbs up for the left side. The penguin ornaments that were stuffed in a ceramic stocking played poker with Top and Mitten.

Total chaos! Lo thought.

Fortunately the toy soldiers maintained their ranks and stood guard, preventing the back ornaments from passing to the front. Seeing them in their places made Lo feel a little better. *At least that's some sense of order,* she thought. *We can't have the back ornaments moving too far forward. That would ruin everything!*

She noticed the inside ornaments peeking out around the toy soldiers. They seemed very frightened. From inside of the tree came the ominous sound of *crunch, crunch, crunch.*

Lo thought, *A crunching sound? I've never heard a crunching sound. That can't be good.*

31

But before she could investigate, Lo noticed Holly checking her hair in a silver ball as she moved around the tree to see how the ornaments were arranging themselves. "Isn't it wonderful to be completely free? To go wherever the spirit moves you?" she said. "No silly rules, no sense of order." She gave a thumbs up to the other ornaments.

"Enough of this," Lo muttered. She shouted, "Hellooo . . . everybody, hello? You've had your fun. It's getting late. Back to your spots!"

Most of the ornaments ignored her. A few glanced her way and went back to their own silly business.

Smiley and Belle swung next to Lo.

"Sorry, Lo," said Smiley. "Wish I could help."

"Me too, Miss Lo," said Belle. "Gracious me, we have to do something before it's too late!"

"I'll take care of this!" Lo shouted as loud as she could. "The party's tonight! Have you lost your minds? What do I have to do to get your attention? Hellooo!" She slammed her paw on a tree branch.

Pop!

The tree lights went out. Darkness was all around her. Everyone became quiet, and there was an eerie stillness throughout the branches.

"Oh no," Lo said, "I didn't mean to do that!"

In the distance she heard the sound of human stomping, and Janice's voice called out, "Don!"

We have to get the lights back on, Lo realized. "Headlight, help!"

Headlight appeared from deep inside the tree. He was a red light bulb, and the leader of a string of lights. His string moved together, bulleting past Lo.

"Ey, Lo," he said in his Brooklyn accent. "I'm on it!"

A white bulb from the bottom intercepted Headlight. It was Whitey, another light with a Brooklyn accent. Whitey screwed and unscrewed himself while talking. "Boss!"

"Which bulb is it?" said Headlight.

"I don't know for sure, but it's prob'ly dem punks on the south side."

"Well, quit screwin' around. Get down there!"

"Okay, Boss!" Whitey screwed himself in and dove to the bottom of the tree.

"You check the back," said Lo, "and I'll check the front."

"*Capice!*" Headlight answered and bolted to the rear.

Lo noticed Otto and Billy on the left side and headed over to join them. She heard noises from the hallway, and the hall light came on. It was the family again. Janice was dashing back and forth as Don rummaged in boxes in the closet.

"I can't believe this!" he said without sticking his head out of the closet. "This is the fourth time."

"This can't be happening now," said Janice.

"I'm done with this tree! It's a pain." Don continued to search through the boxes. "One light goes out, and they all go out. How does that still happen?"

"We'll find it, Don," said Janice.

"There are hundreds of bulbs on the tree. If we don't find it in ten minutes, I'm throwing everything out. Now where are the spare bulbs?"

Ten minutes? That's not much time, thought Lo.

"Throwing everything out? But the neighbors are coming tonight."

"I don't care if we lose the contest," Don replied. "I'm getting rid of this entire tree."

Lo felt herself starting to panic. *We have to hurry. We only have ten minutes!*

CHAPTER 6

As Don continued his search in the closet, Lo looked frantically for the dead Christmas tree bulb. "Everyone, we need to find the bad bulb."

Otto and Billy followed her from branch to branch.

"Look on the other side," Lo said, pointing away. "We don't have much time!"

Otto rumbled, "Zoom zoom!" as Billy hopped onto Otto's roof and they zoomed away.

Lo followed a string of lights, checking each bulb down the line on the light string that circled the tree. There were many strings of lights, and it would take time to search every bulb. But Lo knew what to look for; she knew that a bad bulb was a dirty bulb. All the bulbs looked fine so far, but it was dark around the tree, so she asked each bulb in turn, "How you feeling?"

One bulb answered, "Feeling good."

She moved on to the next. "Everything working here?"

"Not getting any juice," said the next bulb. "But my circuits feel fine."

Lo went to the next and the next and the next, moving on down the line. *How much time is left?* she wondered. She wasn't sure. It was easy to lose track of time with the tree being dark and the pressure on.

Somewhere in the house a dog barked.

Not Ruffy, she thought. Ruffy was the family pet, a Yorkshire Terrier who was always getting into trouble. The previous year, when he was still a puppy he'd thought all the lower ornaments were his toys. He was older now, but Lo still didn't trust him.

Through the branches Lo saw Ruffy trot into the parlor with a rubber ball in his mouth. He followed Don, who now was circling the tree searching for the bad bulb.

"Where is it?" Don muttered.

I hope he doesn't notice us moving around in here.

But Don didn't see the moving ornaments. As he stuck his hands inside the tree checking one bulb after another, he bumped the branches and the ornaments shook.

A skidding sound came from up above, and Lo saw Scarecrow falling from his branch and bumping the lower branches as he fell. He was coming fast and heading straight for Lo. She swung over to the next limb to avoid him, and she reached out a paw to catch him. But Scarecrow fell past her and landed on a colorfully wrapped present under the tree.

It was never good for an ornament to fall from the tree, but Scarecrow was made of soft stuffing so there was no chance of him breaking.

"I'll be right there, Scarecrow," Lo whispered and started toward the lower branches.

But Ruffy had noticed Scarecrow's fall. "Woof!" he barked, dropping his ball and pawing at the presents to get to Scarecrow.

"Ruffy, no!" Lo swung faster, nearly knocking other ornaments from the tree.

Don didn't notice any of this. He was still searching for the dead light bulb.

Now Lo was within reach of Scarecrow. But it was too late. Ruffy burrowed his nose under the tree, opened his jaws, and bit down, taking Scarecrow in his mouth. Ruffy backed out from under the tree and shook his head violently. Stuffing flew this way and that as he began tearing Scarecrow apart.

Lo helplessly watched as Ruffy played with Scarecrow like a chew toy.

Fortunately Janice noticed what was happening. "Ruffy! Bad dog!" She grabbed Ruffy's collar in one hand and Scarecrow in the other.

But Ruffy thought this was a game, and he bit down on Scarecrow even harder. More stuffing came out.

"No! Drop it," Janice said again and again.

Ruffy finally understood and let Scarecrow fall from his mouth.

"You ripped it," Janice scolded. She tried to put the stuffing back into Scarecrow.

Ruffy wagged his tail proudly.

"Mama, can we fix it?" Gina asked.

"Unfortunately, we can't. See, he's just shredded everything." Janice turned to the dog. "You're a menace, Ruffy."

Ruffy sneezed.

Gina said, "Can we hang it on the back?"

"No, honey. No broken ornaments on the tree. Not even for filler." Then Janice said to Ruffy, "Come over here, you. I'll give you your present now. Not that you deserve this."

Ruffy danced with excitement.

Janice unbuckled his old collar and clipped on a new one.

"What does it say on the collar?" Gina asked.

"It says, 'Ruffy.' But it should say 'Menace'!" Janice handed the old collar and the shredded Scarecrow ornament to Gina. "Please go throw these in the trash, sweetie."

"Okay," Gina said and dashed out.

As she watched all this, a wave of sadness washed over Lo. I'm sorry, Scarecrow, she thought. Goodbye.

CHAPTER 7

Whitey was one of the fast bulbs, and he snaked through the south side of the Christmas tree, checking each bulb to find the one that had burned out. The other light bulbs made way, for they knew Whitey was tough. When he came upon a dingy white bulb, he knew he'd found the right one, the Burnout.

"You gotta give me some light!" Whitey said, addressing the dingy bulb.

Burnout didn't respond.

Whitey head-butted Burnout on the left and the right, trying to jumpstart him.

Burnout flopped from side to side without lighting up and his tongue dangling.

"You're a lost cause, Burnout," said Whitey.

Burnout just lay there.

"Have it your way," said Whitey. "I hate to see a good bulb go out."

Whitey peered through the gap in the branches to where Ronnie and Don were circling the tree. They were looking for Burnout. But they were looking in the wrong place, for Burnout was buried deep inside the tree. They'd never find him.

"I need some help here," said Whitey to the other bulbs. "I gotta move Burnout to the end of the branch where the humans can see him. This is no one-bulb job. Teamwork, that's the thing." But the other bulbs didn't respond until Whitey shouted, "Come on! What are you waiting for! Help me push him out!"

With this, some other bulbs joined in, and together Whitey, Green, and Red yanked on Burnout.

"Won't budge," said Red.

"Caught on a branch," said Green.

Headlight joined in, "Pull harder!"

They all pulled. But Burnout was stuck.

Meanwhile, a *crunch, crunch, crunch* came from inside the tree.

"What's that?" asked Headlight as Whitey, Green, and Red shook their heads and their eyes darted back and forth in fear.

Careful not to panic, Headlight snaked past the other bulbs, a lollipop ornament, and a snowflake, searching for the source of the *crunch* sound. As he did, a tree branch *thwacked* him, sending him backward. He cried out, "Yeow!"

Suddenly a voice said, "Pssst! Hey, you."

Headlight spun. "Ey, who's there?"

"It's me," the voice said.

"Who's you?"

"I'm the tree." The tree was alive, and its eyes looked like knots in the tree trunk.

Headlight said, "Hey, pal, look, there's a problem down below. I gotta fly—"

"Me, too."

"Whaddaya mean?" Headlight said.

"I was captured four days ago. The whole lot of us. I was brought to this . . . this . . . encampment."

Headlight smiled. "Oh no, no, you got it all wrong, you're in a house."

"Oh no, the big house?" worried the tree.

Headlight shook his head. "No, not that house."

The tree's eyes darted suspiciously and fixed on the fireplace. "Fire!" The tree saw the burning log, and it thought it must be next.

"Ey, no, buddy—"

"We have to get out!" said the terrified tree.

"It's safe," Headlight assured him. "That fire is only in the fireplace."

"Barbarians!" The tree's left eye started weeping; a drop of sap ran from the corner of the knot.

"Ey, I'm sorry."

The tree sniffled and trembled.

"Did you know him?" Headlight asked.

"Not personally, but we're related," the tree said. "All the trees of the forest are related. Promise me, when we get out of here, you'll plant me back in the ground."

Headlight stuttered, "Er, well . . ."

"Thanks. Name's Yule." The tree extended a tiny branch and touched Headlight's head. "I don't usually make friends with strangers."

"Um, right, I think? I'm Headlight. I got a situation down below, ya know, on one of your big branches."

"I can feel that," said Yule. "So what are you birds doing about it?"

"We're not birds," Headlight explained. "We're lights, see, and there's a dead bulb down there, and we got to get him out."

"A traitor, hunh?"

"Something like that."

"How's this?" Yule moved his lower branch forward.

On the lower branch, Whitey and the other bulbs swung to the front with Burnout.

Whitey said, "Get back!" and they all scrambled to dive back inside the tree—all except for Burnout, who was now hanging in the open where the humans could easily find him.

Headlight said to Yule, "Yeah. That's good."

Ronnie said, "Dad, look at this dirty one."

"Yeah, Ronnie. They're all dirty." But Don took another look at Burnout and said, "I think you found it." He unscrewed Burnout from the string of lights and screwed in a new bulb.

The ornaments and lights scrambled to their spots, and held still, and in a flash the tree lit up.

Janice, Ronnie, and Gina all shouted with glee. "Yay!"

Back on the branch, Headlight gave Yule's branch a friendly head butt. "Great job, Yule, buddy."

Yule winked happily in response.

Lo swung up to Headlight and said, "That was a close one."

"Sure was," Headlight agreed.

"Let's keep it unplugged until we get back," Don was saying.

"Gina, unplug the tree, please, and let's go. We need to get to the Monroes," Janice said. The family left the parlor—all except Gina, who went to the wall to unplug the tree lights. On her way, Gina noticed Lo and stared with a strange look on her face, as if something was wrong.

Oh, no, Lo thought. *Gina knows I moved.*

"Hey," Gina said, her voice full of curiosity. "How did you get there, little one? Mama will not be happy." She reached in and squeezed Lo's glass belly.

Snap!

Lo's golden wings broke off and floated to the floor.

My wings! Tears welled up in Lo's eyes.

Gina gasped and said sadly, "Oh, no!"

The ornaments and lights were paralyzed. They wanted to help Lo, but they couldn't move because Gina might see them.

Lo knew they were all thinking the same thing: Lo's wings are broken. Now she's . . . a broken ornament.

They murmured with shock and sadness.

Gina said, "Little one! I'm sorry, I'm sorry," and she started to cry. She took Lo from the tree and laid her down on the braided rug. Her hands searched the rug as she spoke. "Where are they? Where are your wings, little one?"

Janice called from another room, "Gina, honey? C'mon. We're leaving."

Gina said to Lo, "We have to hide you." She snatched Lo up from the rug, stood, and dashed to the back of the tree, where only a person as small as she was could squeeze between the branches and the wall.

Lo's eyes were fixed and frightened.

"I'm sorry, little one," Gina said. "I didn't mean to hurt you." She kissed Lo's head and hung her in the deepest, darkest place, where none of the humans would see her. "You'll be safe here."

As Gina scampered away from the tree, Lo whispered, "No!"

CHAPTER 8

Lo hung motionless on the back of the tree, her soft eyes darting here and there. She could barely breathe. She heard creepy sounds: strange bird noises and snorting. She'd never been this far back, and the last time she'd seen the back of the tree, the Christmas lights had been on. Now it was dark, and she felt all alone even though she could sense strange eyes around her.

Billy was right, Lo thought. *It is scary back here.*

All the tree sounds were different here in the back of the tree. She heard rustling and murmuring, and not too far away she could hear that *crunch, crunch, crunch* sound again. It seemed to follow her.

She wanted to be with her friends again, with the front-of-the-tree crowd where she belonged. She wondered if anyone even knew where she was. *Surely Janice will see that I'm missing and come looking for me.* But Christmas was a busy time, and Janice wasn't home. Things looked gloomy for Lo. *Scarecrow,* she remembered. *A broken ornament.*

Like me.

She felt bad for Scarecrow, though she hadn't

known him very well.

Now, I never will.

As a broken ornament, Scarecrow had been thrown into the trash. Janice's words came back to haunt Lo: "No broken ornaments on the tree." Crazy ideas ran through Lo's head. *Maybe it's better to hide in the back. It's certainly better than being in the garbage. But maybe Santa's elves find all the broken ornaments, and take them to the North Pole where the ornaments are repaired by the magic of the elves. Maybe Santa hangs the good ornaments on his very own Christmas tree?*

"Santa!" she yelled a little too loudly.

She peeked up at her halo and concentrated. *Please Santa, if you can hear me, please help me. Please take me from this place.* She waited and waited, but nothing happened. *Maybe Holly was right. It's just a plastic halo. It's a fake.*

Lo began to cry. *Poor Scarecrow,* she thought again, but she knew she was crying for herself as well.

As her tears fell, a dragonfly-sized bug swooped by her, and she heard the buzz and felt the whoosh of the wind as it passed. She ducked and stumbled against something hard, a sleeping crusty blue light bulb.

"Ey!" said Blue Bulb. "What the—" He sniffed at Lo. "And who are you?"

Lo stayed silent and avoided eye contact. *I'm not here, I'm not here, I'm not here.*

A plastic elf and a yarn bird whose eyes didn't blink both stared at her ominously.

Blue Bulb edged in. "I'm talking to you, girly!" He snaked around her and pulled her up to his eye level.

She shivered in fright.

Blue Bulb was bad enough, but below her, Ruffy was circling the tree.

"You weren't here before," Blue Bulb said. "Moving to a better spot?"

"No." Lo's voice quivered as she spoke. *A worse spot, actually.*

"Trying to get higher on the tree?"

"No, I, well, this isn't very high."

The back ornaments seemed insulted. Lo noticed lots more of them now. They were starting to crowd around her, checking out the newcomer.

"No," Lo said. "Not that, I mean . . ." *What do I mean?* she wondered. *Pull yourself together, Lo.* She said, "I belong on the front."

Blue Bulb laughed. "There's no way you belong on the front. Look at you. You belong in the trash!" He came closer, breathing heavily on her. "You're busted, kid."

Lo frowned. *It's not my fault I'm broken. Gina broke me. She didn't mean to, but she did it, and she hid me back here. I need to get back to where I belong, which is on the front, not here. Anywhere but here.* "I am not broken. I'm supposed to be this way! We each have a purpose!"

Elf chuckled, showing gold-capped and missing teeth.

Blue Bulb continued, "Nice try, kid. But we've got too many ornaments back here already. You're gonna have to go! Now where is . . ." His eyes scanned the branches below. "There he is!"

Lo looked down. She saw a pink plastic ornament, chipped everywhere, his neck wreathed in a fake string of red and green lights. He had the yellow eyes Billy had spoken of.

Lo knew instantly who this was. She gasped in fear. "Flying Pig!"

"You know him?"

"I, I, I didn't think he made the tree this year."

Blue Bulb grinned. "Don't you just love surprises?"

"Oh I do! I do!" said Todd, a big plain red ball

ornament. He swung himself down and wedged himself between Blue Bulb and Lo.

Blue Bulb said, "Beat it, Jack."

"Jack?" Todd said. "How dare you! Jack is lower than me. See." He pointed down.

They all looked down to where an identical big red ball hung below.

"Whatever buddy," Blue Bulb said.

"Buddy? Well, that's not a bad guess, I guess." Todd twisted and flirted his big ball body. "That lucky son of a gun is on the front. I, however—I am Todd! And quite frankly getting a little upset that you do not know who I am!"

"You're a plain red ball!" said Blue Bulb. "You all look the same."

That's true, thought Lo. The red balls did all look the same, at least to her.

"Not true! I'm as unique as a snowflake." Todd twirled as if to demonstrate his uniqueness.

"This is none of your business, Todd," said Blue Bulb, and he slithered closer to Lo.

But Todd butted in again. "It is, actually. I mean, it is my business."

"Really?" said Blue Bulb. "How so?"

"I'm the leader of the welcoming committee."

"The what?"

Todd sang out, "The welcoming committee!" And in a speaking voice again, he began, "I welcome all ornaments to the back of the tree." Then he whispered, "It's part of the therapy." He spun again and shouted to the others, "Ho! Ho! Ho! We have a new ornament on the back of the tree!" He waved the ornaments over to where he was hanging. "Let's give her a big warm back-of-the-tree welcome!"

The ornaments crowded around and introduced themselves.

"Darlink, welcome. I am Zsazsa," said an old speckled silver ball, with feathers glued to her like a boa. She flicked speckles that showered Lo like confetti.

"Shalom. I'm Dreidel," said another ornament hanging from a makeshift wire hook. He whispered, "Get out while you still can, kid. Before they hardwire you, too."

Elf and Yarn Bird tried to get to Lo, but Zsazsa and Dreidel blocked them. Other ornaments offered added protection. Blue Bulb was surrounded.

"You can kiss this one goodbye," said Blue Bulb, "because she's busted and taking up our limited space."

"Nonsense!" Todd said. "There's plenty of space. And besides, this one is cute. Purple fuzzy head and halo..." He tickled Lo and leaned in to whisper, "You need to do a better job picking friends."

"They're not exactly my—"

"We'll chat later." Todd addressed the other ornaments and Blue Bulb. "Now go, go, go. I need to welcome our new friend to the back."

"You're going to be disappointed," said Blue Bulb. "She thinks she belongs on the front."

Todd burst out laughing. "We can all dream, can't we? Move along, bulbous." He shooed Blue Bulb away. To Lo he said, "What's your name, sweetie?"

"Lo."

"Lo? That's it? Just Lo?"

"Yes."

He shrugged but regained his excitement. "Welcome to the back of the tree, Lo!"

Zsazsa and Dreidel applauded.

Todd said, "Now let me introduce you to—"

In spite of his cheerfulness, Lo began to cry.

"Oh honey, don't cry. This is a glorious day."

"You don't understand!" Lo exclaimed.

"Understand what?"

"I don't belong here! I'm supposed to be on the front!"

Todd looked around at the other ornaments. "We've all heard that one before," he said, and they nodded in agreement.

"But I'm Janice's favorite!"

"No, honey. Janice's favorite is that sweet little ornament with the . . ." He looked at Lo more closely. "With the halo, and . . . oh, my! You? Yes, you! You're the golden one?"

"The golden one?" Lo said.

"The most coveted ornament on the tree," said Todd.

"You know me?"

"Know you! Who doesn't know you? Hey, everyone! Guess who?"

"Todd?" said an oversized psychedelic ball ornament, wearing vintage 1950s sunglasses, labored her way forward. She was chipped and looked as if she'd been hand-painted by a child decades before.

"Wanda?" said Todd.

"Put a lid on it, man!" said Wanda.

"But do you know who this is?"

"Shh!" she shushed. "I know who it is. And if you keep flapping your lips, you're gonna get us all killed, you dig?"

Todd gasped and became quiet.

Lo recognized the psychedelic ball. "Wanda! It's good to see you. "

"I know, baby, I know. How did you get back here?"

"Gina was moving me, and she snapped off my

wings. So she hung me on the back to hide me."

"Outrage!" Todd said.

"Would you hush?" said Wanda.

"Wanda, I need to get out of here."

"I hear you. We all do, before Flying Pig gets word you're on the back. C'mon. I'll take you down to my spot. You'll be safe there."

Wanda eyed the ornaments who were rustling at Lo threateningly.

"You don't understand," Lo said. "I need to get to the front! The party's tonight, the tree's a mess, the front ornaments won't listen to me, and that...that...Holly..."

"Slow down, little one. Who is Holly?"

"Janice gave Gina a new ornament. Her name is Holly. She's very pretty, of course. She was hanging right next to me..." Remembering what had happened, Lo turned away, ashamed. "All the ornaments are listening to her now, to her crazy ideas about hanging wherever you want."

"I like that idea," said Todd.

Wanda whacked him, and he spun on his hook and twisted in some garland.

Lo said, "I need your help. I can't get out of here alone."

"Baby," Wanda said, "this big old ball ain't so fast no more. Stay with me. You'll be safe."

Todd stopped spinning and said, "That would be sooo special! A real celebrity, here in the back!" He was so excited that he began singing.

Zsazsa and Dreidel clinked against each other, excited too.

"I can't stay," Lo said. "We have to win this contest tonight. If we don't, we're all doomed."

"Doomed?" Wanda was wide-eyed.

"Don wants a fake silver tree that spins."

"Say what?"

"It doesn't need ornaments or lights."

"Gibberish!" Todd said. "Who has a tree with no ornaments or lights?"

"There's one across the street."

"Yikes!" Todd said.

Lo turned to Wanda. "If we win this contest, Don will realize we're more beautiful than any metal tree could ever be. So, I need your help."

Wanda shook her head.

"We've waited for this moment all year!" Lo exclaimed. "This is our one chance."

"Ya know what?" said Wanda. "Take Todd."

Todd wrapped himself in garland as she spoke, making a good-looking belt for his big red belly.

"Yeah," Wanda said. "He'll get you to the front."

"But Wanda," Lo begged. "I need you."

"I can't, Lo. I can't go back there."

"Things have changed."

"I'm on the bottom back of the tree every year," Wanda said. "It doesn't get much worse. Janice doesn't even know I'm there."

"We can change that! I promise. Janice will see you and—"

"Todd," Wanda interrupted, "escort Lo to the front, and take the welcoming ornaments with you."

"The front? Really?"

"Really," Wanda answered. "Get moving."

Todd said to Zsazsa and Dreidel, "Let's go. Finally, the front!"

Lo looked at Wanda one last time, but Wanda turned her back as Todd, Zsazsa, and Dreidel grabbed hold of Lo and dragged her away.

CHAPTER 9

As Todd, Zsazsa, and Dreidel escorted Lo toward the front, Lo noticed something odd about the tree. The back branches were oddly angled. Rather than jutting straight out or drooping slightly, they rose upward at a steep angle. In addition, Lo saw only a few ornaments on the back of the tree.

Todd noticed this too and said, "Hey, where is everyone?"

Suddenly Lo realized what was happening. "The tree is tipping!" she said. "The back ornaments are all on the front."

"And I didn't get an invite?"

"The tree is leaning forward from the weight," Lo continued. "We're completely unbalanced. We have to move fast."

"The outrage! I'm going to speak to someone about this …" Todd quickly swung up to a higher branch, glanced out the window, and pointed. "There. Authority."

Lo, Zsazsa, and Dreidel peeked outside where Don,

Janice, the children, and the neighbors were singing Christmas carols. When the song was finished, they all entered Don and Janice's front yard and headed for door.

Zsazsa said, "The humans!"

"They're back," said Lo. "Come on."

Todd said, "Oh you're darn tootin' I'm coming. They're going to get an earful from me about this—"

Before he could finish, Lo yanked him toward the center of the tree.

"Whoa, sister," Todd said. "Not through the center."

"We have to."

"There're crazies in there!"

"We don't have time to go around!"

"Haste makes waste!"

But Lo didn't care, she dragged Todd behind her. Zsazsa and Dreidel followed them into the tree's center, where the atmosphere was dark and shadowy as the four ornaments crept slowly through Yule's internal limbs.

Suddenly Yule shuddered.

Todd said, "An earthquake!"

"You mean a treequake," said Dreidel.

Meanwhile, noises came from within. It was the sound Lo had heard before: *crunch, crunch, crunch.* Something scurried close to them, and a little wet nose startled Zsazsa when it sniffed her from behind

"Run, darlinks, run!" Zsazsa said, and in response, Lo, Todd, and Dreidel turned and ran—*smack!*—right into Flying Pig.

Flying Pig narrowed his evil yellow eyes and snorted, "Fancy meeting you here."

Lo toppled backward and watched helplessly as Flying Pig lassoed Todd with his wreath. The pig squealed happily as he tied Todd to a branch.

As Todd cried out for help, Zsazsa screamed, "You beast!" and swatted the pig with her feather boa.

But Flying Pig, undaunted, moved toward Lo—until Dreidel spun into his way, protecting her.

"Back off, pig!" said Dreidel.

The pig kicked at Dreidel sending him into a wild spin. His makeshift wire hook snagged Zsazsa's feather and tightened. He and Zsazsa wrapped around a branch and landed on it, face down.

But this gave Lo time to right herself and to swing up a branch. Nevertheless, Flying Pig grabbed her and spun her around. Immediately he noticed her missing wings. "Ha, it's true," he squealed with evil laughter, "Janice's favorite little ornament is busted!"

Blue Bulb slithered in. He wrapped his light string around Lo and tightened his grip.

Lo struggled against her bindings. *I'm trapped.*

Flying Pig said triumphantly, "You know what's great about Christmas? We get to clean house!" He flew in circles around Lo. "I've been waiting a long time for this. A very long time."

Still tied to a branch, Todd spoke up. "You're just jealous!"

"Quiet, red ball!" said Flying Pig, and he nodded to the plastic Boston Terrier ornament who swung down to join him.

"I am Todd—" Todd began.

But Boston Terrier stuffed a tiny Christmas stocking ornament into his mouth.

"—I can still talk," Todd mumbled through the stocking.

Flying Pig turned to Lo. "You're busted. You know what that means?"

"It means nothing," Lo said. "Untie me. I need to

get to the front."

"Now, now. Rules are rules," Flying Pig chuckled as he flicked his pig's foot at Lo's halo. "No broken ornaments on the tree." To Blue Bulb, he said, "Push her off!"

"My pleasure," Blue Bulb replied as he unwound his light string from Lo.

He leaned back to shove Lo off the branch, when suddenly—

Whip!

Blue Bulb fell. Plummeting, he knocked into one branch and another, finally falling out of sight.

A large ornament appeared and thrust herself up toward them.

Wanda!

She wedged her large psychedelic-colored body between Flying Pig and Lo.

"I don't think so, Flying Pig," she said.

"Wanda! This is none of your business," answered the pig.

"It's my business, all right. Now back off, or you'll be seeing the worst side of my big psychedelic ball!"

Flying Pig snorted, but he seemed truly frightened of Wanda and he backed away.

"Another time," he said angrily.

"You should be so lucky, fly boy!"

Flying Pig slowly retreated, nodding for Boston Terrier to follow.

When the enemies were gone, Wanda said to Lo, "You okay, baby?"

Lo checked herself and nodded. "Wanda, thank you!"

Wanda replied as she untied Dreidel and Zsazsa, "You're welcome."

They heard a choking sound and looked down to where Todd was gagging on the Christmas stocking.

Wanda said, "Dreidel, go help him."

Dreidel spun toward him, but paused for a moment. "He's a lot quieter this way. You sure we want to do this?"

Wanda thought for a moment, and she nodded.

Dreidel pulled the Christmas stocking from Todd's mouth and placed it on his own head like a silly hat.

"Let's get out of here before they come back," said Wanda.

Lo was surprised. "You're coming too?"

Wanda said, shimmying her backside, eyeing Todd. "Well someone's got to be the muscle around here!"

"I just choose to use my words," Todd said. "It's an option." Then he heard the *crunch, crunch, crunch*.

"Eek!" Todd squealed in fright. The crunches grew louder. The panicked ornaments scrambled in different directions and rushed back together. Slamming into each other, they fell and landed on a large branch at the furry feet of—a chipmunk.

It was an adorable brown and tan striped chipmunk. He had big brown eyes with big puffy cheeks, and the crunching noise came from his mouth as he nibbled a string of popcorn.

The chipmunk offered a morsel of popcorn to Todd with a big smile that showed kernels stuck in his teeth.

"Ew!" Todd said. "How did he get here?"

"You never know what's dragged in with a real tree," Wanda explained.

Dreidel took the piece of popcorn. "I think he wants to be friends."

The chipmunk nodded.

"He's so cute," said Zsazsa, "I love him already." She pinched the chipmunk's puffy cheek.

The chipmunk blushed.

"Okay, little fella," Wanda said. "We're in a rush, so if we could get by you—"

The chipmunk nodded. He scurried up the tree trunk, out of sight, then back down. He did this two more times then stared eagerly at the ornaments.

"Wish I could move that fast," Todd said.

"Wait," Lo said. "We can use him to get to the front."

The chipmunk nodded.

Lo stared into his eyes. "You understand me, fella? Can you take us to the front of the tree? And fast?"

The chipmunk nodded again.

Todd poked the chipmunk in the cheeks. "Let me give you a little tip, cheeks, buddy. Suck those babies in. It'll make you look a lot thinner."

"Let's call him 'Cheeks,'" Lo exclaimed.

The chipmunk nodded yet again, grabbed everyone's hooks in his teeth and dashed away.

CHAPTER 10

They paused to rest in a dark and dank spot in the center of the tree. When they began moving again, Lo crept along the branch holding onto the chipmunk's tail. The other ornaments formed a line behind her: Todd, Dreidel, and Zsazsa, with Wanda guarding the rear.

Without warning, a toy soldier appeared before them.

"Halt!"

They all stopped. Zsazsa and Dreidel cowered.

"I forgot about them!" said Lo. She glanced around her for help, but she didn't know any of the few ornaments that remained here on the side of the tree.

"Easy," Wanda said, leaping forward. "These soldiers can be trigger-happy."

"We'll be fine," said Lo, climbing up over Cheeks. "I'll just tell them who I am."

She dropped down on the branch in front of Cheeks and faced the military line of three toy soldiers. "Hello. I'm Lo—"

Click! They aimed their guns. "Halt!" the lead soldier

said. "No one passes to the front."

"I know," Lo answered in a trembling voice, "and that's a good rule. I like that rule. But I'm a front ornament." She moved closer.

Click! Click! They aimed their guns directly into her face.

Looking down the gun barrels, she froze and held up her paws. "Okay. Not moving." But as she spoke, she heard human voices nearby.

The guests are here for the party, she thought.

In the darkness of the center of the tree, they heard Don's voice saying, "How about some nice warm drinks?"

In response, the guests called out their orders: "Hot chocolate." "Eggnog." "Apple cider."

Lo peered through the branches. She could make out the forms of some of the humans as they grabbed the hors d'oeuvres. At the front door Ronnie was taking coats from newly arrived guests. The door closed behind the last one, and Ronnie struggled with the weight of the winter coats, waddling down the hall as he carried them.

Janice said, "Let's go into the dining room. I've put some more treats on the dining room table."

Don passed a drink to a woman devouring a tiny hot dog appetizer. The round woman had her back to them, but Lo knew who it was from her shape and red hair. *Nana. Janice's mom.*

Don said, "Nana, your drink."

"Thank you, Don." Nana turned and looked directly at the tree. "Your Christmas tree is very full this year."

"We were hoping to win the contest, but the tree is not cooperating this year." He laughed nervously.

"It looks lovely from here," said Nana as Don moved on to pour more drinks.

Lo turned back to the toy soldiers. "Nana is here. I

need to get to the front immediately. She needs to see me."

But the toy soldiers kept their guns aimed at her face.

Frustrated, Todd rolled his eyes and said to the lead soldier in a commanding voice, "You there. Step aside." He pushed forward, unwrapping his garland belt and abandoning it, he muttered, "The depths to which I must sink."

The soldiers *clicked* and aimed their guns at him, but Todd paused, smiled, and pretended to be a tour guide. "And over here we have the center of the tree."

"Halt!" said the leader of the toy soldiers.

"Halt yourself. I belong here. Look around."

The toy soldiers turned, noticing other plain red balls that looked just like Todd.

"And please," he said, "do not point. It's rude!"

He used his hook to lower their guns, and he ushered Lo forward. Wanda, Zsazsa, Dreidel, and Cheeks crept along behind them.

"After the center of the tree you have the front," he continued in his tour-guide voice. He motioned toward the front and waved his hook to get the others to play along.

"Oooh, ahhh," said Wanda in response.

"The front. Yeah!" said Dreidel

"Very nice," Zsazsa said.

"And a little bit further," announced Todd, "is the coveted spot. Front and center."

Click! Click! All the guns were now aimed right at Todd's eyes. Suddenly he pointed up with a startled look on his face. "Look! A flying, ugly, black, something with wings and fangs—oh big fangs!—coming right at us!"

The soldiers raised their guns, searching for whatever Todd had seen.

As they did, Cheeks grabbed Lo's hook and took off.

Realizing they'd been fooled, the soldiers took aim at Cheeks and Lo but Todd flopped on a branch and swung in front of the soldiers. He thrashed about and babbled, "Blue, green, orange, red, white."

The soldiers looked at him and at each other, confused.

Todd continued to babble, and Wanda explained to the soldiers, "He's deranged! Get water! Hurry! Not much time! Please, please, you must save him!"

Used to following commands, the soldiers scrambled to find water.

"Water?" mumbled Todd with a disappointed look. "A gingerbread cookie would really do it for me."

Wanda smiled and watched the chipmunk's fluffy back end disappear toward the front of the tree with Lo behind him.

CHAPTER 11

Arriving at the front of the tree, Lo found a party in full swing. All the ornaments were dancing. Holly, rocking out in her go-go boots, swung her blond hair wildly. Pickle, with no sense of rhythm, did a pickle dance. Belle, Smiley, Headlight, and Whitey were tied to a branch with tinsel and gagged with garland; Pixie and Gnome stood guard over them. Most of the ornaments were clumped together around what had been Lo's spot.

Suddenly Yule's branches bent almost beyond their strength, and the tree tipped forward. The ornaments screamed and held on tight.

"Whoa!" yelled Pickle.

"What's going on?" said Holly.

"We're tipping," Pickle answered. "Maybe we should spread the love by spreading out?"

"Nah, we're fine. I like the angle." replied Holly.

And so, with the tree tipped dangerously forward, the party continued. Meanwhile in the next room, the human guests were having their own party, singing

Christmas carols: "Fa la la la la, la la la la!"

Lo couldn't believe her eyes. The tree was a mess. No way would they win the Christmas tree contest with all this disorder and confusion.

She moved forward, confronting Pickle. "Stop dancing!"

"Why? This is fun!" He turned to see Lo. "Hello, Lo. Where've you been?"

"Never mind," she said. "The human guests are here."

Pickle turned and peered into the next room. His eyes went wide, and he froze in mid-dance. "The guests are here?!"

"Who was on lookout?" But Lo didn't wait for an answer. "No one, apparently." She swung up, landing behind Holly. "What have you done?"

"Hunh?" Holly turned and saw Cheeks. "Animal! Run!"

The other ornaments spotted Cheeks, too, and they screamed, scrambled, and bumped into each other. Holly darted back and forth, looking for an escape. Lo grabbed her as she passed. "The guest are here, and this tree—just look at this tree!"

But Holly was too frightened to listen. "Are you crazy, Bear? Run away! Run for your life."

All the commotion was causing the tree to tip even more. It was now dangerously close to falling over.

"Stop! We're going to fall!" Lo shouted.

Holly dashed behind Lo for protection against Cheeks, crying out, "It's a, a, a furry beast!"

"He's not a beast. He's cute and harmless," Lo said. "His name is Cheeks."

Cheeks licked Holly's face and blinked his big brown eyes.

He was truly irresistible, and Holly's heart nearly melted. "Cheeks?" Holly said, smiling. "I guess he is kinda cute, in a furry, beastly way."

"We need to move everyone to the back," Lo said, "before this tree falls over."

The ornaments didn't move, however. They ignored Lo and looked to Holly for direction. But Holly said nothing and petted Cheeks.

Meanwhile, in the commotion Pixie and Gnome had abandoned their posts, looking for places to hide from the "furry beast." This had left Belle, Smiley, Headlight and Whitey unguarded.

Lo whispered, "Cheeks, buddy, can you gnaw off that tinsel?" She pointed to her four friends tied to the nearby branch.

He nodded excitedly and dashed to help. His sharp teeth cut right through the tinsel bindings, and Lo's friends were soon released.

Now Lo got back to the business of the tree. "Top, you go to the side. Tug Boat, I need you lower. Snowman, down three branches. Bicycle Santa, go to the top—"

"Whoa, whoa, whoa." Holly waved her hands wildly. "I don't think so, Bear."

"We need to win this contest if we all want to see another Christmas."

Holly rolled her eyes. "Again with the contest! You are so superficial. I have a better plan: Christmas spirit."

"Christmas spirit? And how are you planning to bring Christmas spirit to this mess?" Lo tried to move around Holly so the others could see her. "Get out of my way."

Holly refused to move. "You've had your time in the spotlight, Bear. Now it's my turn!"

"Get out of my spot," Lo said, and as they jockeyed

for position, Belle spoke up.

"Shh!" said Belle. "Listen."

Lo paused, and she heard the noises in the dining room.

"Don," Nana was saying, "please plug in the tree."

"Mom, you're going to love it this year," said Janice. "Come see."

Lo didn't have a good view of the parlor or the dining room, but looking over Holly's shoulder she caught a glimpse of movement by the humans. Nana and Janice were heading for the parlor.

"They're coming our way," Lo warned in a whisper.

Don's younger hippie brother, Randy, was chomping on mini-meatballs. "What's up with the real tree, Bro?" Randy asked.

Don shrugged. "I don't know."

"Where's that cool aluminum tree I hooked you up with?"

"It's in the basement. No one knows about it yet. I was hoping to put it up before the party, but that didn't happen."

"Yeah, that would've been way cool."

By now Janice and Nana were in the parlor. They stood staring at the tree. Janice had a strange look on her face. "Don!" she cried. "The tree's going to fall!"

Nana scrunched up her face, but she said in a pleasant tone, "Well, dear, this is an . . . an interesting design . . . with the ornaments and garlands."

"I don't know what happened." Janice took a step back and crossed her arms. "I swear this tree has a mind of its own."

She shook her head, stepped up to the tree, and began re-draping the garlands, untangling the clumped tinsel, and rearranging the ornaments.

Don dashed into the room. He shook his head, disgusted. "Ugh, this tree!"

He tried to straighten the tree, but the weight was still uneven, tipping it toward the front.

Annoyed, Janice said, "Just plug it in."

Don reached for the outlet and plugged in the electrical cord. The tree lit up. But the colored bulbs and ornaments were still clumped in a twisted mess.

Meanwhile most of the guests had moved into the parlor behind the family. They stared at the tree, confused by the disorganized array of ornaments.

Nana said, "Ah, well, hmm . . ."

"Who did this?" Janice asked.

"Guess you're not going to win this year," said Randy.

Don shook his head again.

"Where's your little ornament, honey?" asked Nana.

Janice searched the tree. "I don't know!"

The outer end of the front-and-center branch was clustered with ornaments, and they crowded Lo back toward the center of the tree where she'd never been seen. As Lo heard Nana's words, she tried to push past Holly to get to the front, but Holly blocked her.

"Janice is looking for me!" Lo whispered, struggling to pass Holly.

"This is my moment, Bear!"

"Your moment?"

Janice's hand parted the branches. "Where is my little ornament? Gina? Gina?"

But Gina—the culprit who had broken Lo and put her on the back of the tree—was hiding in the corner behind the parlor's black recliner.

"Watch this," said Holly. She reached around her back to where the pull string was.

"No one's impressed with the pull string," said Smiley.

"Pull string?" Holly reached into the back of her dress. "Ha! I can make this tree shine all by myself! I don't need any of you!"

Under Holly's dress was a tiny black switch. She flipped the switch, and her dress lit up, glowing brightly with a rainbow of colors.

As she did, all of the other ornaments exclaimed, "Oooh!"

Startled and half-blinded, Lo staggered back.

"Now that's impressive," said Pickle.

The human guests noticed Holly's bright dress, and they murmured among themselves: "Wow!" and "Look at that ornament!"

With this, Gina popped out from her hiding place. "Nana, that's my ornament."

"She's very pretty!" Nana said.

Holly swished her dress back and forth, soaking up the attention. "See, Bear, this is how you bring Christmas spirit."

Lo slumped. She couldn't bring herself to watch.

Belle whispered, "You're still the most special, Miss Lo."

Wanda, Zsazsa, Dreidel, and Todd emerged from the center of the tree. "Oh, to sparkle like that!" Todd said as he used his hook to knot himself a sharp looking necktie with a piece of garland. "I'd give my right arm."

"You don't have arms," said Dreidel.

Suddenly Holly's beautifully lit dress turned off. "Hey! What happened?"

"I knew it," Todd said. "A flash in the pan."

Holly reached back and flipped her light switch on and off.

Lo took this opportunity to swing past Holly and head for her front and center spot.

Holly whispered, "Get back, Bear!" She elbowed Lo and turned to grab a sleeping white bulb.

"Ey!" said White Bulb. "Put me back."

"Work with me," said Holly. She put White Bulb against her dress to make it glow.

Lo, still jostling for position, shoved Holly, making her swing outward. Holly pulled White Bulb along with her.

Pop!

The tree went dark.

"Oh, no!" Janice said.

"The lights. Again!" Don complained.

Holly glared at Lo. "Look what you did!"

"Me?" said Lo. "He probably came loose! Screw him back in."

Holly fumbled with White Bulb.

"For Pete's sake," Lo said. "Righty tighty, lefty loosey."

She tried to turn the White Bulb with her short paws, but she couldn't. Holly grabbed the bulb from the other side, and they twisted it together and screwed it in.

Yule lit up.

The sudden flash of bright light startled the two ornaments. "Whoa!" said Lo and Holly together. Falling back, they both swung wildly. Then their hooks connected and became entangled. They flip-flopped and plummeted to the floor.

Lo felt the needles of the tree brushing past her as she fell. She hit a Christmas present, bounced off it, and landed on the rug. Looking up, she saw Holly falling and bouncing off the tree branches, tumbling and turning and growing bigger in Lo's sight until—

Ooof! Snap!

Holly landed right on top of Lo.

"What was that?" asked Janice.

"I don't know," Don said.

But Nana noticed the fallen ornaments, pointed at them, and cried out, "Janice!"

Janice followed Nana's pointing finger with her eyes. "Oh, no, no, no! My little ornament!" A horrified expression came over her face. She reached down, moved Holly aside, and took a good look at Lo.

Lo knew something was wrong with her, but she couldn't imagine what it was. She'd never felt this way before, but she knew that whatever it was, it wasn't good.

"Her belly's cracked," Janice said. "There's a hole on the bottom, and . . . and . . . her little halo is snapped off."

Lo felt Janice's warm teardrops rained down as Janice bent over her.

Gina lifted Holly into her small hands, but no one noticed.

"Hon, I'm so sorry," Don said.

"How did this happen?" Janice asked.

The guests gathered around Janice, but no one spoke.

Pickle whispered, "There goes Christmas spirit."

Janice gently picked up Lo's glass shards. "I'm so sorry, little one. I don't know how this happened to you after all these years." To Nana she said, "I was always so careful."

Lo thought, *This can't be happening.*

Nana reached out and rubbed Janice's back.

"Christmas will never be the same," Janice said, stroking Lo's teddy bear head.

"It's okay, hon," Don said, "I can fix her."

Yes! Lo thought. *That's the answer! Now I know everything will be all right. Don can fix things. I've seen it. Don can fix anything.*

"No," Janice said, her eyes full of tears. "Pieces are missing."

"But I can!" Don insisted.

Janice shook her head. "You might as well get that stupid aluminum tree." She turned and walked away from everyone, and Lo felt herself being carried out of the parlor and through the dining room to the kitchen. Then they stopped. Lo was confused. She'd only seen this room from a distance while hanging from the tree. Everything looked different from inside the kitchen.

"You were so precious to me," Janice whispered, kissing Lo. She nestled her wet cheek against Lo's cracked belly. "I'll always remember the joy you gave me every Christmas."

Lo heard an eerie, metallic *squeak.*

"Without you, there is no Christmas." Janice kissed Lo a final time, and gently placed the broken ornament in the trashcan, on top of the smelly garbage.

The lid smashed down, and darkness enveloped Lo inside the metal can.

Lo cried out, "No! Wait!" and again, "Wait . . ."

But Janice's footsteps faded away to silence.

CHAPTER 12

Lo lay inside the metal trashcan staring up at the closed lid. It was almost completely dark, with only a tiny bit of light streaming in from the edges of the lid above. She heard the sound of Janice's footsteps receding, and other sounds, too. The metal walls of the can made the outside noises louder, but it distorted them. She could hear things in the house, but she couldn't understand what she was hearing.

Is that the roar of the fireplace? Is that a kitchen fan? That electrical sound must be the refrigerator, yes? What is that scraping? A tree branch on the window, maybe? It was all so confusing. Lo tried not to listen to the sounds outside, but they echoed and mixed together inside the trashcan.

It smelled terrible, too. Bits of old food were beginning to rot. The stench was almost more than she could take.

Lo noticed that it was a little warmer inside the can than it had been in the kitchen, but she didn't understand why. Lo didn't understand anything about this place. There was only one thing she understood, and that one thought ran over and over again in her mind: *I'm broken.*

Moments passed. She heard footsteps approaching. The lid rose, and a beam of light flashed across her face. "Yes!" she called out, "I'm here!"

Looking up, she saw Gina's face above, but Gina didn't seem to see or hear her. Instead, Gina hovered her hand over the trashcan and lowered something into it. In the dim light, Lo couldn't make out what it was.

"Friends forever," Gina said, softly and sadly. "Now you can keep each other company." Then she closed the lid.

Boom! The sound of metal on metal echoed inside the can.

In the blackness came a voice. "Ew! What is this place?" It was Holly.

Lo rolled her eyes and then squeezed them shut. She'd had enough of Holly.

But Holly got to her feet, and she stomped on the trash, reacting to the goo underneath her.

Lo rolled, turning her back to Holly. She stared into the darkness, listening to all the terrible sounds, and tears fell from her big brown eyes. "This can't be," Lo murmured. "I'm thrown out?"

Holly stopped stomping. "Thrown out? Maybe you're thrown out, Bear, but not me."

Thump, thump, thump! Lo turned slightly to see Holly jumping and clawing for the rim.

"Too high," said Holly. "I need something . . ." Holly kicked at the scraps of food and named the things she saw among the garbage. "Scarecrow's stuffing . . . Ruffy's old collar . . . pieces of broken ornaments."

Lo turned back over. "I'm a broken ornament."

"Yes, you are," said Holly.

Holly found a small soggy food box with a picture of butter on it. The box was open, empty, and partially crushed. Holly leaned it against the metal wall.

Lo sat up, suddenly angry. "Twenty years of hanging on a tree with no problems. Then you come along, and suddenly I'm in the trash!" She spotted her halo in the mess beside her and put it on her head. It fell off. She put it on several more times, refusing to give up.

"Don't blame me," said Holly. "I'm in here because of you."

Lo ignored her and thought hard about her situation. After a moment she realized that at a time like this, only one person could help—Santa.

She spoke into the halo. "Hello, Santa. It's Lo. Please come, I need help."

Holly blurted out, "And everyone was getting along just fine until you, little miss control freak, came back."

"I am not a control freak!" Lo barked at Holly. Then into the halo she said, "Santa, you've got to get me out. I'm in the trash!"

But Holly grabbed the halo and flung it away. "You are a control freak, and you cannot call Santa!"

"I can call Santa!" Lo searched for her halo.

Holly ignored her and pounded on the metal walls of the trashcan. "Help! I need to get out of here!"

Something fell and bounced off Lo's cheek. She looked down and saw it was a pea. And then, the trash beneath her began to move!

"What's that? What's happening? The ground is moving!" Lo spun in every direction trying to see what was going on.

A twisted string of lights wriggled free from the muck. An ancient light bulb limped forward, dragging his string of bulbs.

Lo squinted to see in the darkness.

The old light bulb coughed between words. "Bickering won't help."

Lo recognized the voice at once. "Greenie! I had no idea!" She hugged him with her stubby paws.

"It's okay, Lo," he said wistfully. "It was time. Headlight's your main light now." Greenie studied the depth of the trash. "You need to get out of here, and fast, little one."

"Fast isn't fast enough for me," said Holly.

"It doesn't matter, Greenie. I'm done. I'm broken."

"Lo," Greenie said, "the trash is almost full. Don will empty it soon, and then we'll all be outside. Once we're out there, there's no way back into the house."

Holly pushed past Lo. "Old man, do you know a way out of here?"

"Yeah, I know a way out."

"What is it?" Holly demanded.

"You two need to work together."

"That's never going to happen," Holly mumbled.

Lo and Holly turned their backs to each other.

"I'm not going," Lo said.

"See?" said Holly. "She's not going. So tell me how to get out of here, 'kay?"

Greenie snaked away. "Work together."

"Ya know, fine. I don't need anyone's help." Holly turned away from the two of them and began piling up food beside the metal wall.

"What are you doing?" Lo asked.

"I'm building a ramp."

A short while later the ramp was completed, and when Lo heard human voices, Holly climbed up the ramp. She was able to push the lid up and peek out into the kitchen. Greenie snaked up the trash ramp, and he peered over the edge, too.

Lo heard the voices again, and she climbed up the ramp and crowded in next to Holly and Greenie. Looking out into the kitchen, she saw Don and Randy enter the kitchen from the hallway. They were carrying boxes.

"What are they doing?" asked Holly.

"Those are the ornament boxes," Greenie said.

The three watched Don and Randy stack the boxes. The two men began to speak.

"She's just so upset, Randy," said Don. "I'd like to throw this whole tree out right now."

"Bro," said Randy, "tell you what. Why not just do that and go with the aluminum one in the basement?"

"Now?"

"Why not? It'll be a surprise."

"Yeah, that's a good idea. But I'll wait until tomorrow. Janice is going shopping tomorrow with the kids. I'll do it then and surprise them when they get back."

"Totally cool."

"I hope it will cheer her up," Don said. "She's still crying over that little ornament."

Lo's eyes widened when she heard this.

"I could have fixed it for her," Don continued. "It would've saved this Christmas. Now I don't know what kind of holiday we're going to have. It's sad."

"Bro, she'll forget all about it when she sees that awesome aluminum tree. You want help putting these back?" Randy said, indicating the boxes.

"Nah," said Don. "I'm going to throw out all the ornaments and lights. We don't need the boxes now."

Suddenly, the trash lid came down with a crash, and Greenie, Holly, and Lo tumbled backward into the garbage.

"He can't do that," said Holly. "Tomorrow's

Christmas Eve!"

"He can do anything." Greenie turned to Lo. "You have to get back on that tree."

Lo glared at Holly. "Send fancy pants. She's the new favorite, with her flashy dress."

Holly rolled her eyes. "That's right, I am. No one needs you, Bear. I can make any tree shine all by myself!"

Greenie said to Lo, "But you're Janice's most beloved ornament."

"She threw me out," Lo said. "I'm broken."

Holly climbed back up the ramp, pushed the lid up again, and peeked out over the rim. "I think he's getting ready to throw the trash out," she said. "Get me out of here, old man!"

Greenie stared intently at Lo, "Lo, with you back on the tree, Don won't have the heart to throw out the tree and all of the other ornaments. He won't disappoint Janice again. You must save everyone!"

But Lo was unconvinced. She touched her cracked belly, saying, "I don't know, Greenie. I don't think I can bring Christmas spirit to the tree looking like this."

Greenie shook his head. "It's not how you look, Lo!" He paused, "I'm disappointed in you. I thought you knew what Christmas spirit really is."

Lo blinked, unconvinced. She knew that Janice favored certain ornaments and that the newest and glitziest ornaments hung on the front of the tree.

Greenie circled Lo and dragged her to the top of the ramp, "Please go. Make that tree special again. Save everyone! Save Christmas!" He turned his wise old face to Holly. "And you, help her. Got it?"

"Me?" said Holly. "No way!"

"Do you want to live to see another Christmas?"

Holly hesitated. "Is that a trick question?"

"Lo is the only one who can make that happen for you and for the others. Janice adores Lo!"

Holly thought about this, and finally she reluctantly nodded. "Fine."

"Good. Now, get ready to jump!"

CHAPTER 13

In the parlor and the dining room, the human guests were putting on their coats and preparing to go. No one was talking. No one was smiling. No one was spreading Christmas cheer. Everyone was somber and silent.

On the tree, Belle was in tears, "Miss Wanda, what on earth do we do?"

"We go get Lo," said Wanda with determination in her voice.

"What good will that do?" said Pickle. "She's cracked."

"A little tinsel goes a long way," Todd said as he wrapped himself making a tinsel skirt.

"You heard Janice," said Wanda. "Without Lo, there's no Christmas."

"But Janice took Lo away." Pickle frowned. "Into the kitchen! And she hasn't been seen since. Janice must have put her in the trash!"

"Lo is the only one who can save us now," Wanda said. "If she's on this tree, Don will not throw us out."

"Ey, Wanda," said Smiley in his baritone voice.

"How can we get into the kitchen?"

Then they all heard: *crunch, crunch, crunch*. It was Cheeks, the chipmunk, munching on popcorn.

Wanda smiled. "I think we just found our ride."

Cheeks could move faster than any of the ornaments. He had the quick, strong, powerful legs of an animal, and he'd trained all his young life running up and down trees, and along branches, and jumping from limb to limb. He was built for speed.

Soon the rescue team was on its way, with Headlight's cord secured around the chipmunk's neck as Cheeks scurried along the perimeter of first the parlor, and then the dining room. He moved fast, darting, pausing, darting again. Sometimes he sniffed to get his bearings and then moved in a new direction. His chipmunk cheeks were puffed out enormously, and in those cheeks were the outlined shapes of Wanda and Todd being carried in his mouth. Headlight stared straight ahead, while Whitey rode on the chipmunk's tail and served as the rear guard. Both were on the lookout for the family dog, Ruffy.

At last, the rescue team crossed the threshold from the dining room into the kitchen. Once in the kitchen, Cheeks spat out the ornaments. Wanda and Todd rolled on the kitchen floor, covered in goo and popcorn kernels.

Todd picked bits of popcorn from his belly with his hook. "Is there no end to this humiliation?"

"There it is!" Wanda pointed to the trashcan. "We have to move fast."

As she spoke, the lid of the can rose as Lo and Holly pushed up on it, struggling to get out.

Headlight spotted them through the space between the lid and the rim of the can. "There they are!"

"Quick, let's go," said Wanda.

But just as Cheeks was about to make his move for

the trashcan, there came the unmistakable sound of a man's footsteps.

"It's Don!" said Todd.

Headlight pulled his cord tight to stop Cheeks from dashing to the trashcan, as Don stepped into the kitchen. He had a newspaper in his hand, and he spread it on the floor. He opened the trashcan lid and pulled out the large paper bag. He tipped the paper bag onto its side and laid it on the newspaper. Lo and Holly tumbled and mixed in under a mountain of food scraps. Don rolled up the newspaper, and began wrapping the trash like a giant burrito.

"No!" said Wanda.

"What is he doing?" Todd asked.

"He's tying up the trash!"

"But Lo's in there! Do something!"

As Headlight scanned the kitchen, searching for a solution, Cheeks unhooked Headlight from his neck and scampered across the floor toward Don.

Wanda called out, "Cheeks, wait!"

Don was on all fours on the floor, bundling up the trash and tying it with twine. Cheeks scurried across his hands. Don screamed, and bolted back. "What the heck?" He swatted at Cheeks. The chipmunk snapped his teeth at Don. Don swatted again and sent Cheeks tumbling.

The twine wasn't quite tied yet, and the string slipped loose. The newspaper opened, spilling out some of the trash. Lo and Holly rolled out.

"Hurry!" Holly yelled, grabbing Lo's hook.

Cheeks jumped on the spilled pile of trash to pull Lo and Holly free. But Don was too fast for them. His hands moved quickly and wrapped the newspaper around the trash. "Gotcha!"

Cheeks was trapped inside with Holly and Lo.

Wanda cried out, "Cheeks!" as Don grabbed the bundle and stormed out to the breezeway.

"What do we do now?" Todd said.

As he spoke, Ruffy pranced into the kitchen.

"Look out!" screamed Whitey.

Ruffy's little black nose bumped into Todd, Wanda, and Headlight.

Headlight scowled at Whitey. "I thought you were on the lookout."

"I was, Boss," said Whitey. "I yelled, 'Look out!'"

Meanwhile, at the sight of the dog, Wanda and Todd were panicking. "Run!" shouted Wanda, and she and Todd hooked onto Headlight's cord. "Hurry!"

With Todd and Wanda in tow, Headlight snaked out of the kitchen, into the dining room, and toward the parlor, heading for the tree. That was the only place where they'd be safe from the mischievous dog.

Whitey dragged behind and swatted at Ruffy's snapping jaws. But Ruffy was playful and quick, and he thought it was all a game. He dodged Whitey's attacks, caught up with the ornaments, and took a really good nip at Todd.

"I am not a chew toy!" Todd yelled. "You overgrown rat!"

Ruffy snapped again, and scraped his teeth along Todd's belly.

"I've been gouged!" Todd said, "I'll never be on the front!" He looked down at his belly and found a deep scratch. Todd scolded Ruffy, saying, "You can't buff these things out, you know!"

Headlight finally reached the parlor and zoomed as fast as he could for Yule with Ruffy in hot pursuit.

On the tree, Pickle saw the rescue team running for their lives.

"We got action at twelve-o'clock!" he shouted.

The tree ornaments cheered.

"Oh dear, c'mon, Mr. Headlight!" said Belle.

"You can do it!" said Smiley.

"Ja, zoom, zoom!" said Otto.

Yule flung out a bottom branch and Headlight latched on. Yule whipped Headlight, Whitey, Wanda and Todd onto the tree. "Yule! Buddy!" Headlight said.

"You left me?" said Yule.

" Eh no, no, no, I would never do that. We stick together, you and me." promised Headlight.

They head butted.

"But where's Miss Lo?" Belle asked.

Wanda stared at the front ornaments and shook her head in the direction of the window.

The rescue team, Pickle, Belle, Smiley, Billy, and Otto all swung to the top of the tree to peek out the window.

Outside, Don carried the garbage bundle toward the giant garbage can. Bits of trash and gobs of goo trickled out of the bundle, including Cheeks who wiggled himself free. But Don didn't notice and tossed the bundle into the can, slammed the lid down tightly, and carried the big can to the sidewalk. After heaving it into place, he smacked the lid again with his fist to secure it tightly.

Seeing him, Wanda's big round belly trembled in despair. "Without Lo on this tree—"

And pickle added, "we're doomed."

CHAPTER 14

Lo and Holly were in the darkness together, surrounded by stinking, filthy trash. This garbage can was large and plastic. Lo couldn't hear much through the walls, but they rattled loudly as Don pounded on the lid above.

"What's he doing?" Holly said.

"Making it harder for us to get out," Lo answered.

In the dark Lo heard Holly cry, and she felt a moment of compassion. Holly was difficult, that was certain, but she was newer and less aware of the ways of the world. They were in a tough spot, and Holly was much less prepared than Lo to deal with problems.

Lo puzzled over their situation, and suddenly an idea came to her. "I know how to get out of this."

"How?" Holly said. "We can't open the lid."

"It will open. We just have to wait, and be ready."

"How do you know this?"

"It happened to my friend, Wanda. The psychedelic ball ornament? She was thrown out years ago, and she escaped the trash. In the morning, a truck will come with some men. I've seen them through the window many times. When they tip the garbage can to dump us into the back of their big truck, that's when we make our break. But you have to stay awake and be ready, okay?"

"Okay," said Holly, but she sounded unconvinced.

A few hours later, the sun broke over the cold horizon. It was the next morning. Lo was startled awake by the noise of a garbage truck screeching to a halt. A rumble shook the trashcan.

"Holly!"

"Hunh?" Holly muttered sleepily.

"Wake up! I think this is it."

Footsteps crunched in the snow.

The lid popped off, and daylight flooded into the garbage can.

Lo and Holly squinted against the bright light.

The garbage can jolted and rose into the air.

"Get ready to jump!" Lo said.

She and Holly held hands, terrified.

The garbage can tipped over. The trash inside began to move from the bottom of the can. A mountain of garbage was heading right for them.

"Now!" Lo said.

As the trash rushed out of the garbage can, Lo and Holly jumped.

They flew through the air, narrowly missing the edge of the garbage truck, and landed on the ground.

Lo felt coldness all over her. She was buried in snow.

She poked her head up and looked around. Above them was the giant truck, a row of houses, and a slight rise in the level of the snow where the sidewalk should be.

"We missed the sidewalk!" she said to Holly. "Hurry!"

"Which way?"

"Um . . ." Lo looked left, right, and under the garbage truck. There were houses all around them, on both sides of the street. She'd never been out here before. She wasn't sure what their house looked like from the outside. "I don't know. I don't recognize . . ." But no sooner had she spoken than she spotted the aluminum tree in the third-story window across the street. "That's the house!"

"Over there?" Holly tugged Lo in that direction.

"No. That's the house across the street." Lo swung Holly around with her hook to show her a white house closer to where they were. "This is our house."

"What now?" shouted Holly.

Holly had legs like a human and could run much faster than Lo, so Lo held tight to Holly's hook, saying, "Go! Run!"

Holly dashed toward the sidewalk, dragging Lo through slushy snow.

They reached the curb, smiled proudly at each other, and gave each other a high five.

"Let's do this," Lo said.

As Holly dragged Lo past some garbage that had fallen from the garbage can, a shadow loomed over them. Lo looked up to see a huge shovel diving toward them. The garbage man scraped the shovel under the snow, scooping up bits of trash—along with Lo and Holly. The shovel flung Lo and Holly through the air. "Aargh!" Holly screamed. They crashed inside the back of the garbage truck, landing hard on a pile of trash.

A metal door swung down.

Boom!

Everything shifted, and as the trash jostled, Lo fell back. The garbage truck was driving away. The truck continued down the road, stopping and starting. More trash rained down on them, and they had to keep digging themselves out. Soon the truck was full of trash.

Beep, beep, beep.

The truck was moving in a different direction now. It was backing up.

"What's happening?" Holly asked.

"I wish I knew."

The truck finally stopped moving. The back door opened, and the floor rose at one end. Garbage tumbled and churned and fell from the truck onto an enormous pile on the ground. Lo and Holly tumbled free, riding the garbage and trying to stay on top of it, until they landed on top of a mountain of trash.

Looking around, Lo saw trash in every direction with other garbage trucks adding more and more. The place stank terribly, and birds circled overhead, screeching and occasionally diving for pieces of rotting fruit or stale bread.

"Ew!" Holly said. "What is this place?"

She and Lo shook with the vibration of bulldozers and dump trucks. Lo recognized these vehicles as huge versions of the little toys Ronnie had gotten for Christmas a few years before.

Holly sat up. Her long hair was frizzed and messy. A banana peel was draped over one side of her head. Her dress was crushed and soiled. Her battery had tumbled out. "Oh, no!"

Meanwhile, bulldozers were moving the trash piles into even bigger piles. One bulldozer was coming their way.

"We have to get out of here," Lo said.

"Look at me! I'm a mess!"

"That's just shocking."

"It's shocking for me," Holly said. She was on the verge of tears.

The nearest bulldozer ground its gears and

approached, its big bucket raised high. It was coming right toward them.

"Run!" shouted Lo. She snagged Holly with her hook and pulled.

The bucket descended inches from them, shoveling forward a heap of stinking trash.

But Holly flopped face down and refused to move.

"Get up! C'mon, Holly!" Lo insisted.

But Holly was depressed. "My beautiful dress," she said, eying her reflection in a twisted metal spoon. "Look at my hair!"

"It's going to look worse if you don't move!"

The bulldozer pressed closer, pushing a mound of garbage like a tidal wave before it.

As the bucket rose again, Lo and Holly fell backward. Broken toys, a plastic frog, and a mangled clown all tumbled free.

The clown landed in front of Lo, and his clown eyes sprang open. "Yeowie kazowie! Hey there, boys and girls! Welcome to the circus here at the dump! Where croaking—" He squeezed the toy frog and it croaked. "—ain't joking! Ha, ha!"

He slapped his knee, and his lower leg popped out and whacked Lo in the face.

"Stay back!" Lo ordered. Grabbing a chicken bone, she stabbed at the clown. "Back!"

"Aw, now," the clown pleaded. "Violence never solved anything."

"I'm warning you." Lo turned to Holly, and spoke through gritted teeth. "Get up. Now."

But Holly didn't move.

"Oooh," said the clown. "A warning. That's some tough talk. Come with us. We help broken toys die. It'll be fun."

Frog croaked. Other toys nodded, zombie-like.

"I am not a toy!" Lo said. "I am a Christmas ornament, and I need to get home before Christmas. I'm special."

The clown laughed, "She's special," and the broken toys nodded with amusement. "Everyone was special, once," he said. "Then you get broken. And you're not so special any more. Just like you." He pointed to the gaping hole in Lo's belly.

"No!" Lo said. "That's not true. You don't know the whole story."

"Yep, everyone's got a story."

The broken toys surrounded Lo and Holly and began creeping forward. Lo jabbed the chicken bone at them, turning herself in a circle to keep them all back.

The clown slithered up to Holly. "Ready to die?"

He opened his lips and teeth wide. The inside of his mouth was gooey and black.

"Ew!" Holly made a scrunched face. "That breath! That'll kill anyone. But we really are special, and we need to get home. Now!"

The clown lunged for Holly.

She dove, and the clown just missed her.

"Clowns are creepy!" Holly said. "Who likes clowns anyway?" She grabbed Lo, snatched a raggedy belt out of the trash, buckled the belt around herself and Lo, and hopped onto a slinky toy.

The bulldozer scooped up more garbage.

Just as the clown and frog moved to attack again, Holly pushed the slinky into motion. The slinky bounced end over end, taking Lo and Holly for a crazy ride.

Garbage fell from the bucket, burying the clown, the frog, and the broken toys. The bulldozer scooped again. Lo and Holly held on tightly to the slinky as it threw them end-over-end down the mound of garbage.

Lo felt dizzy, but she couldn't help but ask Holly, "Suddenly you're special again?"

Holly, also dazed, mumbled, "I have a low threshold for bad breath . . . and spinning rides."

Lo and Holly rode the wild slinky together, flipping and flopping over mountains and valleys of trash.

"Hang on!" cried Holly.

"To what?"

The ride was crazy and bouncy and finally they were thrown off the slinky together. Lo flew through the air with Holly right behind her.

They fell straight toward a gravel path and—*smack!*—landed face-first.

Lo and Holly managed to stand up, and they shook the dirt off themselves.

"Now what?" Holly asked.

Lo looked around. All she saw was huge wasteland of garbage and even more garbage. "I don't know," she said.

CHAPTER 15

Back in the parlor, someone was moving Yule. He didn't sway or vibrate, but he rose high into the air and was moved out of the room.

The ornaments swung wildly, and the light bulbs weren't fairing much better.

"Where are we going, Headlight?" asked Yule.

"I don't know, buddy. Once the tree is in the stand, that's about it until—well, you know . . ." Headlight didn't want to think about what happened to trees when Christmas was over. Instead he yanked his bulbous head higher to get a better look. "It's Don! He's dragging us!"

Wanda shouted, "Hang on, everybody!"

"I can't!" Pickle screamed. "I'm a goner!"

Don dragged the Christmas tree out of the parlor, through the kitchen, and out the back door. While Don focused on the heavy work of moving the tree, Ruffy slipped through the door and scampered out of the yard.

The temperature outside was below freezing, and new snow covered the ground, just in time for Santa.

As Don dragged Yule down the steps with a sharp *bump, bump, bump,* several ornaments lost their grip and fell from the branches. A bus ornament crashed onto the frozen ground. A ceramic stocking smashed. Gold and silver balls plopped, breaking into pieces. Don dragged the tree through thick snow to the edge of the street. He propped it against a four-foot fence and went back into the house.

The ornaments and lights were quiet. Yule, on the other hand, was excited. "Whoo hoo! I'm outside again! Smell the air, Headlight, smell the air!" With one of his branches, Yule whacked Headlight in the back of his bulb. But Yule's nose wrinkled as he smelled something. "Is that smoke?" he asked in a panicky voice. "I smell smoke."

"It's okay, buddy," Headlight said. "I don't see any open flames. It's probably just from someone's chimney. You're going to be fine. I promise."

Yule sighed in relief. He trusted Headlight's word.

Headlight turned to Wanda, "What do we do?"

"We need a miracle," Wanda said. And she shook her head sadly.

The day wore on, more snow fell, and the ornaments and lights grew colder and colder. Hours passed. The snow became heavy, settling in fat white gobs on Yule's needles and branches.

"We have to do something," Headlight said finally. "Maybe we can move the tree by leaning it."

The ornaments were skeptical, but Wanda said, "It's worth a try. And maybe if we move around on the tree, we'll get warmer."

Wanda assembled the ornaments on the forward side of the tree and called out to them, "Lean, lean, lean."

Ornaments and lights leaned forward. Yule teetered back and forth.

"Headlight," Yule said.

"Yeah, buddy?"

"Something's wrong. I can't feel my roots."

Headlight whispered to Wanda, "We have to hurry." To Yule, he said, "It's going to be fine. We'll get you some water, but right now, we need you to hop!"

Yule leaned and hopped, and between the leaning and the hopping, they all managed to get the tree away from the fence and back into the yard through the front gate.

Zsazsa pointed. "Darlinks, look at the pretty lights."

The other ornaments and lights saw them, too. In other yards up and down the street, outdoor Christmas tree lights twinkled.

"We were pretty like that once," said Todd. "No one throws out a lit Christmas tree."

With these words, Wanda's eyes brightened. "Headlight! We need light!"

"Can't do it without the juice, need electricity," Headlight said.

Wanda pointed to the house. "Maybe near the porch?"

Headlight saw an electrical outlet on the outside wall below the porch.

"We're on it!" he said. "C'mon, Whitey. To the wall!"

Headlight and Whitey jumped down from the tree and snaked their cords rapidly through the snow.

Back on the tree Pickle heard human voices. "Anybody hear that?"

Billy was nervous. "Wa-Wa-Wa-Wanda!"

Two raggedy men in dark tattered jackets, one tall and one short, approached and grabbed Yule by the trunk.

"Help!" Yule cried.

"It's the dump people!" Pickle screamed.

The tall man said to the short man, "Yeah. This is a good one. C'mon."

The short man said, "Sure it's big enough?"

"It'll keep the fire burning for a couple of hours."

The men dragged Yule toward the front gate.

"Fire? Burning?" Yule said, panic rising in his voice. "Help!"

"They're going to burn us!" Pickle said.

Headlight and Whitey had almost reached the wall when a sudden tug yanked them backward.

"Headlight," said Whitey, "they've got Yule!"

"Keep going, Whitey, I'll try to stop 'em." Headlight doubled back to Yule, leaving Whitey to trudge onward. He quickly found the short man.

The short man saw Headlight coming, but he couldn't believe his eyes. "What the—?"

Headlight wrapped his cord around the man's leg, tangling and tripping him.

As the short man fell back in the snow, the tall man laughed at him. "Ha, ha, two left feet, ey?" He propped Yule up and reached out a hand to his short friend.

"That cord grabbed my leg! Did you see?"

"You're crazy."

Meanwhile, Whitey had reached the wall. He plugged himself into the outlet, and the Christmas tree instantly lit up with bright colors.

The men were stunned. "Whoa," said the tall man.

The short man's eyes went wide with fear. "It's cursed!"

"Cursed? It's beautiful." The tall man's face glowed happily in the colorful lights. "I haven't had a lighted Christmas tree since I was a little boy."

He straightened Yule, and he piled snow around

Yule's base to keep him standing upright.

"What are you doing?" said the short man. "Let's get outta here!"

"That's better," said the tall man. "Hey, I got you something."

"What?"

The tall man dug into his pocket and pulled out a broken pencil. "I know you like to write."

"For me?" A smile broadened the short man's face. "Thank you." He hesitated, looking embarrassed. "I, ah, I didn't—"

"It's okay. You don't need to get me anything," the tall man said. "Let's leave this tree right here. It's too pretty to burn."

The short man nodded. "You know what? You're right. Merry Christmas, Stan."

"Merry Christmas, Lou."

They turned and moved away, arm in arm, helping each other walk through the deep snow.

CHAPTER 16

Holly dragged Lo by the belt through the garbage dump. They'd been moving along for hours. It was dark, the area was full of bad smells, and the ground beneath them was treacherous, sliding and moving unpredictably. Many times they tripped or stumbled, and they had to keep picking themselves up.

"I'm so tired. I can't go on," Holly said breathlessly.

"You have to," said Lo.

"We're traveling in circles."

"No," said Lo. "It's just that all the trash looks the same."

Holly stopped. "It's over, Bear. Let's face it. We can't find our way out of this dump, and even if we did, we have no idea how to get home."

She sat, dejected, and unbuckled the belt. Then she tossed it aside.

Lo refused to give up. "We have to try."
Determined, Lo rolled herself over and grabbed the belt. It

flipped, and the metal buckle smacked her nose, making her eyes water. But through her tears, she could see writing on the metal tag. Lo read it out loud: "RUFFY 54 VEAZIE STREET." She thought for a moment and then exclaimed, "Ruffy!"

"What? Where?" Holly spun around.

"No, he's not here. But this is his old collar." She showed it to Holly. "It must have been thrown away in the trashcan with us after Janice gave him his new one."

Holly was unimpressed. "Goodie, that'll get us home. We can ride on the magic collar."

"Don't you see?"

"See what?" Holly looked around her. "I see garbage. I see snow. I see you. And I'm not fond of any of it!"

But Lo was so excited she didn't hear Holly remarks. "The numbers and letters. It's our address!"

"Hunh?"

"The address. Where our house is. We just have to figure out how to get back there." As she spoke, Lo noticed a smokestack in the distance. "There!"

Holly glanced up, not sharing Lo's excitement. "That smokestack. There's smoke coming out."

"So?"

"There must be people there," Lo said. "C'mon!"

"Ugh, really?"

"Yes! C'mon!" Lo reached out a paw to Holly.

Holly rolled her eyes, bothered by the thought that she had to pick Lo up again. She stared down at Lo's short paws begging to be picked up. "How does a Bear not have legs?" Finally, she hoisted Lo up with Ruffy's collar, and they headed for the smokestack, with Holly doing most of the work.

"Watch out!" Lo hollered as a bulldozer thundered

across their path.

Holly stopped short, tumbled away from the bulldozer, and rolled into a pair of blue-and-white polka-dot legs stuffed into yellow booties.

They both looked up and straight into the old eyes of a doll with platinum hair pulled into a bun at the top and a pair of bifocals hanging of her nose.

"You may call me Granny," said the doll. "Would you like to play?"

Lo screamed. Holly yanked Lo away and tripped over a dusty old toy locomotive.

Granny reached down for Holly and Lo. Noticing Ruffy's collar, the doll took it in her hands, and her eyes scanned the tag.

Lo protested, "We need that!" She lunged for the collar, but Granny yanked it away.

"Do you want to hear a secret," asked Granny.

"Give it back," Lo demanded.

"If you could have three wishes, what would you wish for?"

Lo tried again, but it was no use. Granny held the collar high and out of their reach. Without the collar, they didn't have the address, and they'd never find their house. Lo felt defeated. "I just want to go home."

Granny eyed something in the distance. She placed Lo and Holly on the locomotive.

Holly said, "What's going on?"

The train said, in a Mexican accent, "Loco take you for a ride."

"Loco?" said Holly.

"No!" Lo said. "I want to go home, now!"

"Si!" said Loco. "Su casa! Arriba! Arriba!"

Loco tooted his steam engine, played cha-cha music, and motored over the clumpy, filthy ground, following

Granny to the main office of the garbage lot. The two toys and the two ornaments paused at the door and peeked into the office where men's work boots tramped back and forth.

"What are we doing?" asked Lo.

"Si, we have to wait for the men to clear out. We don't want to get seen."

The four of them waited until the men had left the office. Granny quietly entered and walked over to a wall. On the wall was a map of the city with all the street names below it in alphabetical order. Granny scanned it carefully, peered at Ruffy's tag, and looked back at the map.

Lo and Holly sat on Loco, staring up at the map. Lo saw a red dot labeled: "YOU ARE HERE."

Granny pointed to a street on the map.

"What?" Lo asked. "What is it?"

"Would you like to try on my glasses?" Granny asked.

"I don't need glasses," Lo said. "I just need to get home."

Granny was pointing at "VEAZIE STREET."

Loco said, "Señorita, that is the street named on the tag."

Lo wobbled to the wall and studied the map closely. "Can you take us there?"

"Si, Loco can!"

Holly looked through the doorway. She saw something outside and grabbed Lo. "Bear, we do not have time to ride on a toy train."

"Then how will we get home?"

"The U.S. Mail," said Holly. "It's very reliable!" Holly pointed through the doorway at a mail truck idling by the gate.

"How do you know it's reliable?"

Holly said, "I was shipped by U.S. Mail, and I arrived

just in time for Christmas!"

"Right," said Lo. "How could I forget?"

"See? You need me, Bear."

Lo checked the map again.

Holly continued, "Okay, good? You know where to go?"

"Yes," said Lo. "I have a photographic memory."

"Of course. Remind me to make a list of all the things you can do."

Lo smiled, and they both heard crunching footsteps outside in the snow. The mailman was heading for the mail truck.

"Hurry!" said Holly. "Let's go!"

Granny put Lo and Holly on Loco, and he chugged out to where the mail truck sat with its engine still idling. The mailman opened the side door and climbed into the truck. Loco zoomed up to the rear bumper, and Granny followed him. When they reached the truck, Granny lifted Lo and Holly onto the bumper.

"Thank you, Granny," Lo said.

As the doll nodded, from out of nowhere a little girl's hand swiped at Granny, grabbing her and raising her high into the air. Lo and Holly went flying. They smashed to the ground, and even more bits broke off of Lo.

"There you are!" the little girl said to her Granny doll. "How did you get out here?"

The girl had red ribbons in her curly golden hair, and she wore a plaid skirt. "Daddy's going to be mad that you left the office," she said as she walked away carrying her doll. She pulled Granny's string, and Granny said, "Oh my dear, you are getting to be such a big girl!" As the child disappeared into the office, Granny hung over her shoulder and waved to Holly and Lo.

As she did, the mail truck gunned its engine. Holly

grabbed Lo and tossed her onto the mail truck's bumper. Lo swung her hook down. "Grab on!" Holly grabbed Lo's hook, and Lo lifted her up just in time.

The mail truck sped away, carrying the two little ornaments down the dark, snowy street.

CHAPTER 17

The mail truck surged forward with Lo and Holly riding on its back bumper. Cold wind whipped around them as the truck jostled and swerved. But Lo ignored all this and focused on the names of the streets they passed: Oak Street, Elm Street, and Maple Street.

"You know where we're going, right?" Holly said.

Lo said, "Um . . ."

"You're scaring me, Bear. Do you know where we are?"

"I'm not sure!" Lo admitted.

"What happened to 'I have a photographic memory?'"

"I do have a photographic memory, but these street names don't look familiar."

The mail truck bounced as it hit a pothole. Lo lost her grip and slid off the bumper, but she managed to secure her hook again and narrowly avoided falling. She looked down at the slushy blacktop racing by below. The door latch above seemed loose, and it rattled with each bump.

The mail truck hit another pothole, and the back door swung open, knocking Holly from the bumper. She fell from the speeding vehicle and landed head first in a snowbank.

Lo cried out, "Holly!" and as she did, the truck suddenly stopped. Lo flew up and forward, slamming into the half-opened back door. The vehicle parked with the engine running. The front door opened, and the mailman got out. Icy slush crunched underfoot as he stepped toward the back.

Lo jumped into the snowbank below, landing in the wet coldness. With slow effort she rolled to where Holly had landed. Holly's head was still buried in the snowbank by the side of the street. Only her feet stuck out of the snow.

"Are you okay?" Lo asked.

"Do I look okay?" said Holly in a muffled voice. She kicked her feet in the air, trying to free herself.

Using her hook, Lo pulled Holly from the snow.

A few feet away, the truck's back door slammed shut. As the two ornaments turned to hop back onto the bumper, the truck's tires spun, flinging gobs of heavy wet snow and burying Lo and Holly. Then the mail truck sped off down the street.

Holly dug herself out and noticed Lo's hook sticking up out of the snow. Lo struggled, swinging her hook back and forth, but she couldn't get out. Holly stared at her for a long moment, but eventually she pulled Lo out.

"Thanks," Lo said. "I thought you were going to leave me."

"It crossed my mind."

Holly dusted the snow off her dress and then, as she looked past Lo, her eyes widened in fear.

"What?" Lo asked.

Lo spun around and came face-to-nose with—the furry snout of a dog!

As the dog sniffed at Lo she wanted to run away, or roll away, or fly away. She wanted to do whatever it took to get away from the hideous beast, but she was frozen with fear.

The dog opened its mouth wide, and its jaw clamped down on Lo, not tightly, but firmly enough to get a good grip on her. Lo felt herself lifted up from the snow.

Holly ran, but the dog chased her, Lo dangling from its mouth. When the beast caught up with Holly, it snapped at her. Lo fell from its mouth, but it snatched up Holly by her head. "Help!" Holly cried.

Lo grabbed her by the legs and hung on as the dog took off running. It scampered down the street, running in and out of parked cars. A truck turned straight into the dog's path. The dog tried to stop short, but it slipped on the ice and slid under the truck, spinning and skidding safely to the other side.

Dangling below the animal's jaw, Lo pulled on Holly's legs, vainly trying to free her from the slobbery jaws.

"You're going to pull my head off!" Holly protested, but her voice was muffled inside the beast's mouth.

"That wouldn't be the worst thing that could happen," Lo muttered.

The dog hopped a curb, ran at full speed down a sidewalk, turned a corner, passed through a gate, and stopped in someone's backyard. It barked, spitting out its passenger. Lo and Holly dropped to the snow-covered grass.

"Moof, moof, moof," barked the dog.

Holly wiped dog spit from her face. "Ew!"

Lo glanced around and saw more houses. They were

in a backyard with a fence, but it could be anywhere. "Where are—"

"Arf! Woof! Woof! Woof!"

Lo rubbed her tired eyes and looked closely at the dog. Something about its face seemed familiar . . . Then she recognized him.

"Ruffy?" She looked at the backyard again, and at the back of the house. "He brought us home!" she cried excitedly.

"Home?" In addition to being disgusted by the dog's slobber, Holly was confused. Lo said, "Good boy, Ruffy!"

"We're home?"

"We're home!"

Holly and Lo hugged.

"I love that dog!" Lo said.

"We made it!" said Holly. She shook her head with a gleam in her eye. "Thanks for not giving up." And with those words, they hugged again as Ruffy looked on.

"Woof! Woof! Woof!"

"Let's go save our tree!" said Lo.

Holly winked and took hold of Lo's hand. They ran up a step to the back door, but suddenly—

The door opened with a whoosh!

It crashed into Lo and Holly, sending them both flying through the air. Holly fell to into the deep snow, but Lo flew farther, straight into a hole in a wall, an old dryer vent.

She landed inside what seemed to be some kind of tunnel. She tumbled down the vent in the dark. *Clink! Clank!* She flipped end-over-end and came out in the basement where she landed on a cardboard box.

The box had lettering on it. Dizzy from the fall and the landing, Lo's vision was blurry. But nevertheless she could read the words: "REAL OLD ORNAMENTS."

The words got blurrier as Lo felt dizzier.

She began to lose consciousness, and as she fell against the box, her world went black.

CHAPTER 18

Holly was still outside, stuck in the snow. They'd made it back to the house, but now she couldn't find Lo.

"Bear? You there? Lo?"

There was no answer.

Holly heard Don's footsteps in the yard as his boots crunched on the ice and the slush.

"Ruffy?" he said in a voice that echoed through the neighborhood. "Ruffy! Get in here now!" He paused and called again, "Ruffy!"

Dog barks came from around the corner of the house, followed by the sound of paws running. Ruffy skidded to a halt in front of Don.

"There you are," Don said. "Back inside, you crazy dog."

Ruffy moved in and sniffed at Holly.

"It's too cold out here to play, and there's nothing to hunt—hey!" Don stood directly over Holly, looking down on her. "Ruffy, good boy! You found Gina's ornament." He bent down and lifted her from the snow. "How did you get way over here?"

Holly wanted to roll her eyes to the back of her head and tell him all she and Lo had been through. Instead, she shut her eyes tightly against whatever might be in store for her.

"Let's get you back where you belong," Don said, and holding Holly in his hand, he moved through the back door and into the kitchen.

As he carried Holly, she scanned the backyard and began to panic. There was no sign of Lo. She shut her eyes tightly again.

Once inside, Don set Holly down on the kitchen counter. "Ruffy, did you do this?" He straightened Holly's hair, wiped her face and dress, and opened a kitchen drawer. "That hook is crooked. There should be another hook in here somewhere."

Just then the front door opened and Janice and the children entered. They came through the house and into the kitchen, carrying shopping bags.

"Back so soon?"

"Not much left to buy on Christmas Eve," Janice said.

"I have a surprise." Leaving them in the kitchen, he stuffed Holly in his pocket and stepped through the dining room and into the parlor.

In the parlor, he rummaged through a box in the corner, found a new hook, removed her twisted bent one, and replaced it with a new one.

Don held Holly by her new hook and smoothed her hair.

This relaxed Holly, and she opened her eyes. To her great surprise, she saw a different tree, and she nearly fainted. It wasn't Yule standing there in the parlor. It was a metal Christmas tree that spun in the corner and glowed with colored lights as red, green, yellow, and blue washed over it.

"I suppose every tree needs one ornament," Don said, and he hung her on a sharp metal branch.

As the tree spun slowly around, it gave her a view of the parlor, a wall, a window, another wall, the parlor, a wall . . .

Every time she moved, the metal needles jabbed her. "Ouch!" she said. "This has been the worst twenty-four hours of my seventy-two hour life!" She raised her legs, trying something different, but more needles poked her. She scanned her surroundings, and realized she was . . .

Alone.

"Someone help me. Are you there, Lo? Please?"

Janice and the children entered the parlor, and Don and Janice stood in the doorway arch, directly under Missy, the mistletoe.

As the tree spun slowly around, Holly could see the family only when it spun her to the front, looking out into the room. But she could hear the family talking, even when she faced the wall or the window.

"Now the kiss," said Missy said to the stockings. "Get ready."

The stockings, hung by the chimney, nodded.

"What do you think?" Don asked.

Ronnie saw the tree and exclaimed, "Wow!"

"Daddy, where'd you get that?" Gina asked.

"I had it in the basement."

"Really?" Janice said with no enthusiasm in her voice.

Missy twisted her branches eagerly. "Here it comes."

"Randy got it," Don said, "and I thought, you know, since our other tree was a disaster . . ."

The tree spun, and Holly came into view again. She

107

saw Janice nodding sadly.

"It's cool!" Ronnie exclaimed. He ran up to the metal tree.

Gina pouted. "I think it's boring."

"But look, honey," Don said, "I found your ornament."

Gina stared at Holly hanging alone on the metal tree. Holly was certain the little girl would take her down and play a game with her. But Gina looked shocked and ran to the kitchen trashcan where she was sure she had thrown Holly out to keep Lo company.

"What do you think, hon?" Don said. "A perfect Christmas tree, hunh?"

Missy grew even more excited, and whispered, "Kiss, kiss, kiss . . ."

But Janice ran from the room and out to the kitchen. She was crying.

Don called out to her, "You said it didn't matter because your little ornament was broken. So I thought . . ." His voice trailed off. A look of disappointment came over him.

Meanwhile Ronnie, bored with the new tree, left the parlor to go play.

Missy said, "Is there ever going to be a kiss in this house?" But the stockings just shrugged in response.

Don stood alone in the parlor, a look of disappointment on his face. "You'll grow to love it," he called out to Janice, but his voice sounded unconvinced.

He left, and Holly said out loud to the empty room, "It's all ruined, Christmas is ruined." And for the first time, tears dripped from her eyes. For now she was all alone.

CHAPTER 19

Lo awoke in the dark. She remembered falling through a narrow tunnel. Before that, she had been outside, in the snow, on a mail truck, at a dump, in the garbage, and on a tree . . .

It all came back to her now.

She looked around but could barely see. Dim light streamed in through a dirty window and from the dryer duct. She recognized it now. She was in the basement, the place where the family kept all the Christmas decorations and ornaments. She was on a box, atop a pile of other boxes. She saw a furnace and a ladder. Looking down, she felt dizzy at the distance to the floor. It was too far to jump.

Thump, thump, thump.

The sound was coming from the box she was on, and it was making the box vibrate.

Someone inside the box said, in an Italian accent, "Lo! My bambina!"

Lo recognized the voice. "Christmas Mouse? Is that

you?" She could hear him but not see him.

"You know it!" said the mouse ornament from inside the box. "Is Christmas over?"

Lo sighed, feeling dejected. "I guess you can say that."

"Was it beautiful?"

Lo felt even more depressed.

"Lo? You okay?"

The lid of the box moved, one corner rising. The lid flaps slanted, and Lo rolled over to another box. She caught herself just before she rolled off and fell to the ground.

Christmas Mouse peeked out of the ornament box. He pushed open the lid flaps and other ornaments appeared: Plastic Donkey, Tear Drop, and Silver Bird. These were old ornaments she had known years before, but most of them hadn't been on the tree for many, many Christmases. Lo was glad they hadn't been thrown into the trash like she'd been.

The old ornaments noticed Lo's broken body, her tattered fur, and her missing halo and wings.

"You don't look so good, Lo," said Christmas Mouse.

Tear Drop spoke up, to make Lo feel better. "Why don't you rest in here until the 'favorites' box comes down?"

"I miss you guys," Lo said.

"We miss Christmas," said Plastic Donkey. "We haven't been on the tree in years."

Silver Bird said, "Do they ever miss us?"

"Yes, they do," Lo lied. "It's just, you know, limited space and all that. I think next year everyone will make it onto the tree."

"You think?" said Christmas Mouse.

"Yes, Janice is talking about getting a bigger tree."

Creak!

The door opened at the top of the stairs. Footsteps pounded down.

Plastic Donkey said, "Hide! Someone's coming."

The old ornaments ducked inside the box and shut the lid flaps over themselves.

Lo panicked, not knowing where to hide. She lifted the top cardboard flap of the old ornament box and rolled underneath.

Don came down the stairs. He went to a blanket on the floor and lifted it to reveal a hidden shoebox wrapped in Christmas paper. Curious, Lo raised the cardboard flap and leaned over the edge to read the writing on the shoebox: "To Janice. Merry Christmas. Love, Don."

As he lifted Janice's wrapped gift and put it under his arm, Lo lost her footing and slipped back into the old ornament box. She fell, coming down on top of Tear Drop.

Tink!

Startled by the noise, Don turned around. "What the heck?"

He went to the ornament box, raised the flaps—and there was Lo!

"Hunh?" he said, lifting her gently and gazing at her with a puzzled expression. "Ornaments are just popping up everywhere!" He looked up through the basement window. It was getting lighter outside; morning was coming. "Who knew a little ornament would have such a big impact on Christmas?"

He grinned and carried Lo up the stairs and into the parlor. Don hooked Lo into the bow on Janice's present and placed it under the metal tree. Then he rubbed his tired eyes, checked his watch, and left the room.

Inches above Lo, sharp needles spun.

"No!" she said. "Yule is gone! I'm too late."

There was a sudden rustling behind her. It was Cheeks! He scrambled down the chimney and plopped into the fireplace, a safe distance from where a few embers still glowed orange-red in the grey ash. The chipmunk had something in his mouth, something with an odd shape. He scurried past a few hot embers, and stopped at the sight of the cold metal tree. His eyes looked sad.

Lo called out, "Cheeks!"

Seeing Lo, the chipmunk bounded over to where she was hooked onto the present beneath the tree. He nuzzled Lo happily.

"I'm stuck," she said reaching for her hook with her short paws. "Can you help me?"

Cheeks nodded. He unhooked Lo from the Christmas bow, and they hugged.

"It's so good to see you!" she said.

Cheeks opened his mouth, and Lo's halo fell out. He nudged it toward her.

"My halo!" she exclaimed. But her good mood quickly vanished. "It's too late, Cheeks. I'm too late."

He nudged the halo again.

"No, it's plastic. Holly was right. It doesn't really work."

Cheeks took the halo in his paw and held it out insistently, waiting for Lo to take it.

She stared at the halo and glanced through the window. Outside the sky was brightening with the promise of a new morning, a Christmas morning.

"Santa," she said, into the halo. "Please come, I need your help." She didn't feel confident as she listened.

Nothing.

Cheeks put his paws on his hips and pleaded with his eyes as if to say, "You need to do better than that."

Lo held the halo between her paws, bowed her head, and prayed. "Santa, of all the wishes in my heart, I wish our tree—our majestic Yule—to come home from wherever he is, along with all the ornaments and lights, so we can bring Christmas spirit to our family."

Cheeks nodded as if to say, "Good job."

At that moment Don returned, his arms full of wrapped presents.

Seeing the chipmunk he said, "You again! Ick!"

Lo called out, "Cheeks! Run!" as Don chased the animal into a corner and grabbed him. He opened a window and tossed Cheeks outside. Cold air and a whirl of snowflakes swept into the room before he closed the window. He added the presents to the pile under the tree before leaving.

Somewhere above her, Lo heard a voice. It sounded like Holly. "Lo? Is that you?"

"Holly?" Lo stared up at the spinning metal tree above her, but she didn't see any ornaments, just colored light.

"Lo! Please help! Get me down from here!"

"Where are you, Holly?"

"I'm stranded on this awful tree! The metal needles are sharp. I can't move!"

The tree continued to spin, and Lo spotted Holly dangling from a metal branch. But as tree turned, Holly quickly moved out of sight.

"Hang on," Lo said. "I'll get you down."

She rolled and hobbled in many directions but couldn't figure out a way to get Holly down. Then she heard another sound.

Click, clock, ting, cling.

Lo searched for the source of the sound, and she saw the old ornaments creeping happily into the room, led by Christmas Mouse. When the mouse saw the metal tree, he exclaimed, "Madonna mia! Lo, what is that thing?"

"It's the worst tree ever! It's ruined Christmas. I'm so sorry. I should've been honest before. We're all going to be thrown out."

"Thrown out?"

"Into the trash."

The old ornaments looked suddenly sad.

"It's okay, Lo," said Christmas Mouse, "we understand."

Holly's voice called out from above, "Someone please help!"

Lo pointed up at the metal tree and explained to Christmas Mouse, "Holly's my friend, and I need to get her down."

Christmas mouse stared up and looked worried. The cold metal branches were dangerously sharp. He nodded and gulped with fear.

CHAPTER 20

The old ornaments worked together, trying to reach Holly on the sharp metal Christmas tree. But the tree was too dangerous. Its knife-like metal needles stuck out from every branch. The glass ornaments were afraid of shattering, and the cloth ones feared they'd be shredded.

"Link together," Lo suggested. "Like monkeys in a barrel."

The ornaments remembered the monkeys-in-a-barrel game and thought it was worth a try. They linked hooks and hands and whatever else they had, and they flip-flopped up the side of the tree with the ornaments complaining all the way: "It stabbed me!" "I'm caught." "Help!" "Ouch!" "I'm coming undone." "That's gonna leave a mark."

Despite the pinches, pokes, and pains, however, they made steady progress on the tree, swinging one ornament up, and another, and another.

Finally Christmas Mouse reached out to Holly. "Grab on!"

But Holly couldn't quite reach. "Too far," she said.

Lo heard footsteps. "Someone's coming! Hurry!"

"I need one more ornament," Christmas Mouse said.

They swung again, sending up Tear Drop, but she overshot Holly.

"Missed," said Tear Drop, as a man entered the parlor. All Lo could see was his big black boots. The man walked toward the metal tree.

Tear Drop slid from the upper tree and scraped all the way down. She grabbed Holly as she passed, saying, "Hop on!"

"I'm sorry it was so painful for all of you," Holly said, "but thank you." She looped her hook onto Tear Drop.

The man in the black boots grabbed the metal tree, lifted it off the ground, and tipped it horizontally. With his other hand, he grabbed the rotating base.

Lo watched helplessly as Holly and the old ornaments dangled from the horizontal tree. "Whoa!" the ornaments said. Sharp needles jabbed them. "Ow!" said one ornament. "Yikes!" said another.

The man carried the metal tree toward a box behind the couch, and as he did, Lo called out to her friends, "Jump onto the couch!"

Christmas Mouse spotted the couch as the tree went past it. "Okay, we got this. Now!" The ornaments all jumped, swinging end-over-end.

Thud!

They landed on the couch in a heap.

The man in black boots put the tree and the rotating base into a big long box behind the couch, closed the lid, and left the room.

Christmas Mouse said, "Everyone good?" They checked each other, looking for cuts and tears and wounds and breaks. Despite a few scratches here and there, they all seemed fine. Together the ornaments swung down from the couch and joined Lo on the floor. And once they were safely on the floor, they looked around them.

Something was wrong. The room was empty. There was no tree.

They heard the back door in the kitchen swing open and closed. Lo squinted through the dining room. She couldn't see clearly, but she could make out that the man in the black boots wore a red velvet coat and a red hat. And he was carrying something very big.

She shook her head in disbelief, rubbing her eyes.

"Lo?" Holly said. "What's going on?"

Lo stared at her halo. "It does work."

The man in black boots came back into view. He was carrying Yule and Yule's tree stand.

And he looked just like—

"Santa?" said Christmas Mouse.

"He must have heard my prayer," Lo said, crying tears of joy and hugging her halo.

"I guess you really can talk to Santa," said Holly, amazed.

Santa lowered Yule into the tree stand and tightened the bolts. But Yule looked weak and droopy. Santa went to the kitchen and returned with a pitcher of water. He poured the water into the base of the Christmas tree stand, and Yule revived slowly. His eyes opened as he took the water into his trunk, saying, "Ahhh . . ."

Lo saw all the familiar ornaments on the tree. They were tired-looking and cold-looking and disorganized, but to Lo they had never looked so good.

Lo's attention quickly shifted to the window where, outside, the first rays of sunlight illuminated the snow.

Holly noticed this, too. "The sun's coming up!" she said. "Let's find our places." She dragged Lo to the tree.

Candy Cane was the first to spot them. "It's Holly and Lo!" He lowered his hook. Holly grabbed it and swung Lo up.

But before taking her place on the tree, Lo said, "Wait!" She turned to the old ornaments from the basement. "Guys, c'mon!"

They looked at each other in surprise. "Us?"

"Yes," Lo said. "Of course. We can't bring Christmas spirit without you."

"We need you," Holly agreed, and so did the newer ornaments dangling on the tree.

By now Yule was coming back to life. "More colorful birds," he said. "There's plenty of room in the back."

The old ornaments scattered around Yule, grabbing onto the low-hanging branches and working their way up and onto the tree.

Headlight looped around Lo and Holly to help them up. "How 'bout a ride, ey?"

Lo and Holly nodded, and Headlight took them to the front and center.

Todd was there to greet them. "Glory be!"

Wanda was there, too. "Lo! Holly! You're here?"

"We are!" said Lo.

"We thought you two were goners!" said Todd.

"We were goners. It's been quite a journey back," Holly said, and she took Lo's paw in her hand and squeezed it affectionately.

"Look, Lo," said Todd, pointing to the window.

The sun had fully risen.

"Time to welcome Christmas morning! Ho, ho, ho!" Todd twirled with excitement.

"Quick, everyone," said Lo, "back to your spots."

Ornaments zigged and zagged, jumped and dropped,

clustered and scattered and smashed together, not sure where to go.

"No, no, no," said Holly, "the spots that Lo put you in."

Lo smiled.

"Great idea!" said Billy as he jumped on Otto's roof. They zoomed to the side.

The other ornaments scrambled to their places.

Just then, Santa plugged in the tree, and Yule shined brightly with beautiful colors.

From the hallway came Gina's sleepy voice. "Santa?"

Santa jerked around and bumped into Yule, who protested, "Whoa, there."

Gina stared at Santa. And Santa froze, like a reindeer in the headlights. "What are you doing, Santa?" Gina asked.

Santa, surprised at being seen by an early-rising child, could only stammer, "Oh, ah . . ."

"That's our tree," Gina said. "You brought it back?"

"Why, yes! I did, Gina." He patted her head with his big black glove. "You know, you were right. That silver tree was boring."

Gina's eyes widened. "You heard me say that?"

"Of course. Santa hears everything."

Gina hugged Santa's leg. "I knew it!" she exclaimed.

"Shh, now. You don't want to wake everyone," he said.

Yule now bore the weight of all the ornaments, both old and new. He drooped and leaned forward, still dizzy from being outside and without water.

"You okay, Yule?" Lo whispered.

"Uh, yeah, I'm good," Yule said, but he didn't sound too sure.

Santa lifted Gina and together they basked in the Christmas spirit brought by the tree and the lights and the dangling ornaments.

"But Daddy's going to be mad," Gina said suddenly.

"No, honey. Your daddy was just trying to make Christmas special. He got confused, that's all," said Santa. "I promise you, this is what he really wants. The magic of a real tree."

Gina hugged Santa tightly. "This is going to be the best Christmas ever!"

Santa lowered Gina gently. "Now I have more work to do," he said, "more houses to visit. You go back to bed."

Gina nodded and scampered away.

Yule began to sway. "Headlight," he said, "something's wrong with my trunk."

"Yule?" Headlight said. "Hang on, buddy."

Yule listed forward.

"We're going down!" Pickle screamed.

Todd yelled, "Save yourselves!"

The entire tree was shaking, and leaning, and about to tip over, and the ornaments were panicking on the branches.

Santa turned toward the tree. But as he did—

Pop! Snap!

The screws were popping off the tree stand.

"Oh, no," said Lo.

"Hang on, everyone!" said Wanda.

And as she spoke those words, the tree toppled right on top of Santa. He stumbled backward. His boots snagged on the braided rug. He fell.

Clang!

His head slammed into the radiator. The tree landed on top of him. Ornaments crashed to the floor.

"Santa!" Lo screamed.

But Santa was out cold.

CHAPTER 21

Lo was trapped under Yule's thick branch.

"Yule, can you lift this branch up?"

No response come from Yule.

Lo struggled to free herself and found an opening. Inch by inch rolled herself out from under the tree.

As she did, she heard Holly cry out, "Lo!"

"Holly! Where are you?"

"Under here."

She followed the sound. Like Lo, Holly had fallen from her place on the tree and was now pinned under a lower branch. Lo tried to lift the branch, but it was too heavy and she couldn't budge it. Lo said, "I'll get help!"

Other ornaments emerged from inside the tree, dazed and confused. The back ornaments were in better shape, for they had ridden the tree down without being trapped under it. All were slowly recovering from the impact.

Lo ran for Wanda, Belle, and Pickle. But they were

not moving.

"No!" Lo said. She searched for help and saw Todd on a branch just above Santa. Todd leapt down from the tree and landed on Santa, who wasn't moving.

"Is he okay?" Lo asked.

"I don't know," Todd said. "I can't tell if he's breathing."

"Listen for a heartbeat."

Todd put his ear to Santa's belly button.

Wrong spot, thought Lo, *though I'm not sure.*

"I can't hear anything!" Todd shouted.

"Move around and listen harder," Lo suggested.

Todd listened at various spots on Santa's chest. "Nothing!" he exclaimed. "We've killed Santa! We've killed Christmas!"

But Lo wouldn't believe it. She dashed over to Santa and climbed on top of him. She shook his fluffy collar. "Santa, please wake up!"

Zsazsa sniffed. "What's that? I smell smoke!"

Lo continued with Santa. "Wake up. I don't care if I'm on the front. I don't care if I get thrown out. Just please save everyone. Save the house. Save Christmas!"

On the floor a red bulb smoldered against the braided rug, and started to burn.

"It's the rug. It's smoking!" yelled Dreidel.

Headlight zoomed toward Red Bulb and smacked it to the left and the right.

Lo leapt down from Santa's chest and tossed aside her halo. She grabbed Red Bulb. *Ow!* It was hot. She tried to unscrew the light but it burned her paws and she couldn't hold onto it, dropping it into a pile of dead pine needles that had shaken loose from the tree.

"Whitey, pull the plug!" Headlight screamed.

Whitey yanked on the light cord, but it was snagged

around a branch and didn't come free from the outlet on the wall.

Then *whoosh*, the needles ignited.

"Fire!" Lo was horrified.

Above the doorway arch, Missy was panicking. "Hurry! I'm a dry branch!"

The stockings by the chimney cried, "We're a nylon and cotton blend!"

Flames spread through the pine needles. The rug caught fire, as did a tree branch. Yule woke up and noticed he was engulfed in flames.

Yule screamed in terror. "Not fire, no!"

"The tree stand has water!" Lo yelled. She wobbled to the stand and used her paws to flick water onto the fire. But it wasn't enough. "Help! Everybody!"

The old ornaments joined her, but they couldn't flick out enough water to extinguish the fire. The flames were spreading and out of control.

"Move the tree stand closer!" said Christmas Mouse.

Headlight and Whitey surrounded the stand, dragging it closer to the fire.

"Tip it over!" Lo said.

They struggled with the stand, but it was too heavy.

From out of nowhere, Flying Pig and Boston Terrier appeared, along with some other back ornaments.

Lo and Flying Pig eyed each other. Then Flying Pig nodded, and together they all pushed the tree stand. It tipped, and twisted, and water poured out—but it missed the fire. Instead, the water splashed onto Headlight and Whitey.

Pop! Pop! Pop!

Headlight's cord shorted out. The bulb went dead, and his entire string of lights darkened.

"Headlight! Whitey!" Lo cried as she struggled to revive them.

The fire crept slowly toward Santa, still unconscious on the floor. Todd waved his hook, trying to blow out the fire, but the light breeze only fanned the flames and made them worse.

Flying Pig oinked, "We need more water!"

Lo spotted the fish tank on its stand with the single goldfish swimming inside. "The fish tank!"

She grabbed ribbons from the burning presents and tied them together. Then she tied one end to Flying Pig's wreath and said to Flying Pig, "Tie this around the fish tank. When I yell 'now,' you guys push. Got it?"

Flying Pig nodded. He threw his wreath, and it caught on a back corner of the tank stand. An army of ornaments scaled the tank stand on a desperate mission.

Lo held the end of the ribbon. She felt the air growing hotter as flames shot up behind her.

Holly had managed to wriggle free, and she limped toward Lo. The heat was melting her dress and go-go boots, and the flames stopped her from getting too close to Lo. She cried out a warning, "Lo, stop. Run. You'll be killed. We need you!"

But Lo knew what she had to do. She had to save everyone and save Christmas.

"You can lead the tree," Lo said to Holly.

"No, I can't!" Holly protested.

"Promise me you'll fix the tree before the family sees it. Promise me!" As she spoke, Lo felt hot flames burning all around her. Her fuzzy head was singed by the fire. "Now!" she said, and she yanked on the ribbon.

Flying Pig and the other ornaments pushed. Lo pulled so hard that she fell backward into the flames. But she saw the fish tank tip and tumble. Water gushed toward her. The goldfish rode the wave down. Lo thought she heard Holly call her name: "Lo!" She heard the sound of glass breaking and water flooding.

And then there was nothing but darkness and silence.

CHAPTER 22

Holly stood helplessly as the fish tank crashed down on top of Lo.

A tidal wave of fish-tank water washed over the flames, dousing the fire. The branches and rug hissed and steamed.

The goldfish flopped on the rug, struggling to breathe. Holly grabbed its tail and put it in a small puddle. Then she splashed over to where Lo lay broken and lifeless.

"We need you, Lo," whispered Billy. "Please come back."

Otto said, "Zoom, zoom, Lo?" He nudged her limp paw, but Lo didn't move. Otto opened his side door and Lo's golden wings fell out and landed beside her.

Billy said, "We found your wings, and have been holding them for you."

Todd leapt off Santa and headed for Lo, crying out her name. "You can have your spot back, Lo," he said. "I was just keeping it warm for you!"

Cheeks scurried down the chimney and tumbled out, covered in soot. He dashed to Lo's side, but she was still broken and unmoving. His big brown eyes teared up.

Another noise came from the chimney, along with a cloud of dust. Suddenly a man was standing in front of the fireplace. He was dressed in a pristine red velvet Santa suit, he had a large bag on his back, and he looked straight at Holly with a twinkle in his eye.

"Hunh?" she said aloud. "Santa Claus?" She looked at the Santa on the ground, and back at the Santa by the fireplace. "Two Santas?"

Meanwhile human sounds headed into the parlor. It was Ronnie and Gina, running.

"C'mon, Ronnie!" Gina said. "I saw Santa. You gotta see!" She and Ronnie barreled into the room.

At the fireplace Santa Claus waved his gloved hand, and Gina and Ronnie froze in mid-stride. They were like statues, not moving, not breathing, as if time were standing still.

Santa Claus by the fireplace turned to the Santa on the floor under Yule. He reached down and pulled off the other Santa's hat and beard to reveal—a familiar man's face.

"Don?" Todd said. "With a fake beard! He's the one that brought us back in from outside?"

The real Santa Claus waved his gloved right hand, and Yule rose into the air and left him hovering above the wreckage. He waved his left hand, and Don rose into the air, floated across the room, and landed gently on the couch, where he began to snore.

Next, Santa surveyed the brunt wreckage.

From his bag he lifted a tiny pouch. He reached in with his fingers and pulled out a pinch of golden dust, which he scattered on Yule. The tree was instantly restored to health, becoming new and fresh once more.

"Hey," Yule said, waking up, "I smell good!"

Santa smiled. "Hello, mighty Yule."

"I, I, I look great!" said Yule.

"You certainly do." Santa Claus winked, spun Yule, sprinkled the magic golden dust on all the lights and ornaments, and lowered Yule into the tree stand.

He stared at the old ornaments. "I haven't seen ornaments like you in years," he said as he sprinkled golden dust on them. They rose into the air and a moment later, they all were gently hanging on the tree.

Christmas Mouse said, "Look at us!"

"We're on the tree!" cried Tear Drop.

"Yay!" tweeted Silver Bird.

Plastic Donkey kicked. "Hee-haw!"

Pickle admired his new shiny coat of metallic green. "Look at me! I never thought this could happen!"

Todd said, "I'm as unique as a snowflake." He twirled, admiring his shiny red paint and brand new glitzy snowflake design. "Who needs tinsel?" and he tossed his tinsel sash aside.

"Never mind you, I'm psychedelic gorgeous, baby, just like new!" said Wanda, dancing and showing off her fresh colors and new sunglasses. She swung over to Headlight. "Give me some skin, brotha."

Headlight's eyes peeked open, "Ey, who turned out my lights?"

Santa Claus draped garland, and with his gold dust he magically lighted Yule.

Poof!

"Your lights are on, my man!" Wanda said, but looking around she noted, "The parlor is still a mess, though."

Almost before she'd finished speaking, Santa sprinkled magic dust around the room, restoring the rug and the presents and the fish tank. Fresh water appeared in the tank, and Santa gently lifted the goldfish by the tail and dropped it back in the tank where it belonged.

As Cheeks sat waiting his turn, Santa saw him and said, "Hey, little fella, I know where you belong." With his big-gloved hands he placed Cheeks deep inside the tree, near Yule's trunk, and slipped him a tiny bag of popcorn. Cheeks munched away happily, watching as everything else was restored.

Holly stayed on the floor next to Lo, holding on to Lo's halo as she watched the many miracles. They were wonderful, but none of them lifted Holly's spirits. Lo was burnt and crushed. Her fur was singed. Holly looked up at Santa tearfully and said, "I only want one thing for Christmas, Santa. Please bring Lo back."

Santa Claus took the halo from Holly's tiny hand. He scooped Holly up and magically restored her dress, her boots, her beautiful hair, and her battery. He hung Holly front and center on the tree. Her dress flashed and she glowed beautifully. Smiley smiled at her.

But still Holly pleaded, "Santa, please help Lo."

Now Santa Claus turned to Lo and scooped her up, gathering her many pieces. Her glass belly was completely missing. "Wake up, sleepy-head," Santa said, and he breathed gently onto Lo's face.

Lo took a shallow breath, gave a short sigh, and one of her eyes peeked open.

CHAPTER 23

Lo's eyes fluttered open. She saw a man looking down on her. He had a white beard and wore a red velvet coat.

Santa Claus, she thought. But she remembered that Santa had been hit by the falling Christmas tree and knocked out, perhaps even killed. And there was a fire and a fish tank and—

"Santa?" she managed to say. "You're not dead?"

Santa Claus laughed. "People say that all the time, but I'm very much alive."

Memories came back to her now, memories of all the terrible things that had happened over the past few days. She thought, *It's all my fault.* "I ruined Christmas," she said.

"Doesn't look like it to me," said Santa. "Look." He gestured at the beautiful Christmas tree in the corner, where the ornaments were all spaced and arranged neatly, along with garland, tinsel and twinkling lights.

It looked perfect and magical.

"Holly," Lo said. "She saved Christmas."

"It was you who saved Christmas," Santa said, and as he spoke he restored Lo's clear glass belly and reattached her golden wings.

"I don't understand, how?" Lo asked. *It makes no sense*, she thought.

"I got your message."

Ting!

The halo appeared above her head. Lo smiled.

"It's not what you say or what you do," said Santa, "and it's certainly not where you hang on a tree. It's how you make others feel. And you, Lo, make everyone feel special."

Santa approached Yule. Holly moved to a nearby branch, and Santa hung Lo front and center.

But Lo turned and began to leap toward the back, saying, "Holly, you were right. The ornaments should hang wherever they want."

Holly grabbed her before she could move. "No, Lo. This is your spot. It will always be your spot. And this—" She twirled. "—is my spot. We all have spots for a reason, right?"

Lo had never before felt so warmly toward Holly. She smiled sweetly at her, and they hugged as the other ornaments cheered.

Meanwhile Santa Claus noticed Dreidel hanging by himself and looking sad. He lifted Dreidel from the tree, removed his wire, and placed him on a satin cloth in a beautiful blue box stamped with a Star of David.

"And here's my spot!" said Dreidel with a smile.

Santa closed the lid and put Dreidel under Yule.

"Santa?" Lo said. "May I have one more Christmas wish?"

Santa Claus nodded.

"I wish for the tree to stand in front of the windows."

Santa gave her a questioning look. "Why?" he asked.

"So that every ornament hanging on the back can be seen, even from the outside."

"Of course, Lo," Santa said with a wink and a grin.

The ornaments on the back of the tree cheered, and everyone recognized the voices of Zsazsa and Flying Pig.

Santa Claus paused for a moment, thinking. He saw, behind the couch, the box marked "ALUMINUM TREE."

"We can do better than that," he said.

With a wave of Santa's hand, Yule rose into the air, out of the corner and moved toward the bay window. The rotating base of the aluminum tree came out of the box and slid under Yule, and Yule descended gently onto it. Santa waved his hand again, and Yule spun slowly and majestically in front of the bay window. Beautiful lights danced and reflected off the shiny ornaments.

As Lo turned past the bay window, she saw the morning newspaper delivery boy outside, trudging through the snow. He stopped and looked up, marveling at the sight of Yule in the window.

"Totally cool!" he said.

Lo smiled the biggest smile of her life.

Now Santa Claus turned to Don, still lying on the couch. Santa threw his golden magic dust onto Don, and in a flash, Don's Santa costume was transformed into cozy pajamas, and the nasty bump on his head disappeared.

Toys rose from Santa's magic sack and flew through the air and into the stockings until all the stockings were stuffed. Wrapped boxes landed gracefully under Yule's lowest branches.

Santa studied the tree, and finally he said, "Merry Christmas, Lo."

"Merry Christmas, Santa," she answered.

He smiled, his red cheeks filled with mirth, and the sound of a hearty chuckle escaped his lips: "Merry Christmas to all!"

The lights and ornaments replied in unison, "Merry Christmas, Santa!"

He reached into his bag again, pulled out a final pinch of magic dust, and tossed it in the air. In a flash, Santa was up the chimney.

Lo heard footsteps on the rooftop, the pawing of reindeer hooves, and the jingle of sleigh bells.

Ronnie and Gina unfroze and raced into the parlor, wearing their pajamas. They seemed not to realize that any time had passed. When they saw the Christmas tree and the ornaments and all the new presents, they stared happily.

"Whoa! Look at our tree!" Ronnie said.

"Pretty, isn't it?" said Gina.

Janice entered, rubbing the sleep from her eyes. Seeing Don on the couch, she gently prodded him awake. "Don? What in the world?"

He awoke reluctantly, rubbing his head. "What?"

"You brought back our tree?"

Don smiled up at her. "Yeah, well, I was hoping . . ." But before he could finish, he noticed the tree. "Hunh?" He sat up, bewildered, blinking and staring.

"It's beautiful," Janice said. She approached the tree and saw Wanda on a lower bough. "My psychedelic ball! I thought you got thrown out years ago."

She kissed Wanda and moved her to the middle. The branch bent under her weight, and a tear dropped from Wanda's eye.

Don said, "I sneak her on every year."

She reached out to hug him. "You do? Oh, Don . . ."

While her back was turned, Smiley and Belle gave

Wanda a wink.

Don took Janice's hand in his. "Your mother told me you made her when you were four. I figured she was special."

"She is." Janice looked at the tree again. "And that's very sweet."

More ornaments spun into view. Janice gazed at the old ornaments with a look of recognition. "And you brought up all the old ornaments!"

"I did?"

"Thank you so much, sweetheart. You really don't mind packing them all up, do you?"

"What? Uh, no, I guess I don't."

Missy the mistletoe grew excited because Don and Janice seemed about to kiss.

Meanwhile the tree continued spinning slowly, and Lo swung into view of the parlor.

Janice saw her on the tree. "Don! You fixed my little ornament."

"I fixed it?" Don was confused, but he didn't argue. He simply rubbed his head and went along with everything Janice said.

Janice cupped Lo and kissed her sweetly, weeping tears of joy. "Thank you, thank you."

Gina pointed to the tree. "Mama, look at Holly. She's brand new, too."

The little girl jumped up and down with glee. As Holly circled and came back around again, Gina reached out to grab her.

"Honey," her mother said, "let's not touch the ornaments, okay?"

Gina pulled her hand away, nodded, and smiled.

Don rose from the couch and moved toward his wife. Taking Janice's hands in his, he led her under the mistletoe and stared deeply into her eyes.

"Finally!" Missy said.

"Now that's a Christmas tree!" Don said.

"Mmm," said Janice, looking dreamy into Don's eyes, "is that Christmas spirit?"

"It sure is. Merry Christmas, my love."

"Merry Christmas, darling."

They kissed, slowly and passionately.

Missy glowed. "Now that's a kiss. Whoo hoo!"

The Christmas stockings nodded.

Ronnie fidgeted by the fireplace. He was impatient, and not just because of the kissing. "Can we open our presents now?"

His parents stopped kissing and laughed like children.

"Of course," Janice said.

The family gathered around Yule, and Gina handed out the presents according to the names on the boxes.

Janice helped her. She lifted a gift wrapped in forest-green paper. Looking at it curiously, she turned to her husband. "Don, I don't know where this came from, but it has your name on it."

"Oh?"

Gina was excited. "Santa brought it, Mama!"

"He must have." Janice turned to Don. "You go first, darling."

He opened his present.

Watching the scene in the parlor, Lo was excited by the Christmas spirit that pervaded the atmosphere. This was what Christmas was meant to be. She reached for Holly and held her hand.

"Friends forever?" Lo said.

Holly nodded. "Friends forever."

Each one squeezed the other's hand.

By now Don had finished unwrapping his unexpected gift. Lo couldn't see it what it was, because she was facing the window now, but she heard Don say, "This is amazing!"

"It's your very own ornament, Daddy," said Gina. "Hang it front and center!"

Holly and Lo glanced at each other. "Hunh?" they said at the same time.

They spun back into view of the parlor, and as they passed by, Don hung the new ornament right next to them.

It was a Paul Bunyan lumberjack.

As they spun toward the bay window, Paul Bunyan tipped his hat to Lo and Holly. "Ladies!"

Lo was instantly smitten, and she noticed that Holly was smitten, too. Lo gathered her composure and said, "Well, ah, hello."

Holly, too, struggled to act nonchalant. "Um, hi there . . . Paul. "

Lo stared at Holly.

"What?" said Holly with a false note of innocence in her voice.

Lo mimicked Holly: "'Hi there . . .Paul'?"

"That's his name."

"Oh, please."

Holly rolled her eyes. "How about your 'Well, ah, hello'?"

"What? I'm welcoming a new ornament to our tree."

Holly crossed her arms. "Uh-hunh."

Paul scratched his head. "Something the matter, ladies?"

"No," said Lo.

"Nothing at all," said Holly.

"Everything's just . . ." They grinned at each other.

" . . . perfect," they said in unison.

Paul Bunyan gave a sly grin. "Because if I'm in the wrong spot—"

"No, no!" said Lo.

"You're in the right spot," said Holly. "Every ornament has a proper spot!"

"Wherever that might be," said Lo.

Holly nodded. "Most definitely."

And with that, Lo and Holly grabbed hands and winked at each other as the beautiful Christmas tree turned slowly and happily around and around.

THE END